I0638578

A Trial of Rock and Rope

Nicholas Licalsi

STEP INTO THE ROAD

First published by Step Into The Road Publishing 2022

Copyright © 2022 by Nicholas Licalsi.

First edition

Editing by Dan Varrette

All rights reserved. No part of this publication may be reproduced, stored or transmitted in any form or by any means, electronic, mechanical, photocopying, recording, scanning, or otherwise without written permission from the publisher. It is illegal to copy this book, post it to a website, or distribute it by any other means without permission.

This novel is entirely a work of fiction. The names, characters and incidents portrayed in it are the work of the author's imagination. Any resemblance to actual persons, living or dead, events or localities is entirely coincidental.

From this point on take everything with a grain of salt. I made most of it up!

For my dad who showed me life can be more than most people make it. I hope you've found your rock.

Thank You Patrons!

You encouraged me to take this story from the blog to paperback. You've helped me every step towards this mountain's peak. Katelyn Combs, Bonnie, BW, Melinda Callender, Roy & Beth Shockey, Callen McMillian, Sam Meeks, Matt VanNatten, John Middleton, and Avish.

Thank you to everyone who read this book ahead of time and gave me feedback on it. You all helped make this book better!

I

Forest

Chapter One

H e waited in line on a sandy beach. Waves rolled in on his left while a tall mountain rose out of the horizon to his right. The only other moving thing was the line as each person took a slow step forward every few minutes.

He asked the people ahead of him what was going on, but they responded with vague gestures and seemed as clueless as him. Everyone wore the same white linen clothes, but it didn't feel like his typical attire.

As he moved forward, he noticed a man with well-groomed white hair wearing flip-flops and a bright red Hawaiian shirt. The man repeatedly disappeared with the person at the front of the line. Soon after, the Hawaiian shirt man would reappear only to vanish with the next person in the queue. To check if he was dreaming, he pinched his arm. It stung, but it didn't convince him he was awake.

The person in front of him then disappeared. On the ground in front of him someone had painted a red X in the sand. Written under it were the words *Stand Here*. It was amazing that the people ahead of him hadn't worn away the markings.

Looking at the X, he wondered how long his time in the line had lasted. It felt like his whole life, but he had only a brief memory of it.

Either way, he was glad it was over and felt excited to see what standing on the mark held for him.

He stepped onto the *X*, and the Hawaiian shirt man appeared, smiled, and stuck out his hand for a shake.

"Hello, Dr. Ferruccio Monteiro, glad you're here."

"Just call me Ferrun," he said instinctually. The name fit better than the clothes. He grabbed the man's hand, grateful for the introduction. Ferrun wanted to ask who the man was and where they were, but before he could ask his questions the ground dropped out from below his feet.

"I'm Merc, the god in charge of orienting you," the man said. The two floated like clouds above a landscape.

"What are we doing up here!?" Ferrun asked. He didn't think he was afraid of heights, but anyone would be terrified looking down at the ground from a mile up.

"This is the afterlife. Well, an afterlife. Specifically, yours." Merc rolled over like he was merely swimming in a pool. "Obviously, it's yours since you're here, but you're sharing this world with thousands of other ascension candidates as well."

"I died? How?"

The man groaned and rolled his eyes. "Everyone wants to know that. Unfortunately, it's above my pay grade to know. I simply supply you with your Divine Trial."

Ferrun squirmed in the air, trying to get comfortable with the fact he was a few thousand feet above the ground without any support. "A what trial?" was all he could sputter out.

"Most of the time your consciousness, the thing that makes you Ferrun, just gets recycled, and parts are passed to other humans who are dragged into existence. It's a messy primordial mix of consciousness. Every once in a while some conditions are met, and people are selected to skip the recycling and are given a Divine Trial like this one. You, and the others here"—he gestured to the trees below—"met that condition."

Ferrun didn't think that sounded like him. Then again, he didn't really remember much before the queue on the beach. "What did I do? Why can't I remember anything?"

"Amnesia is normal. It will come back to you. Not sure what you did. I'm just the messenger, and I have to get on with explaining the Divine Trial. We don't have all day." He cracked a childish smile. "A bit of afterlife humor."

Ferrun returned the smile with confusion and looked down. Before looking away from the terrifying fall, he noticed movement between the trees in the forest below. People were littered throughout the forest, and they were the only sign of life below. Some seemed to be struggling through the woods, while others moved easily among the trees.

"The trial is to get to the peak of that mountain." Merc gestured at the mountain on the horizon. "If you get to the top, you'll ascend to godhood."

"Have a lot of people ascended?" Ferrun asked.

"No one's pulled it off yet, but eternity is a long time. I'm sure that one of you will eventually figure it out."

"What's so hard about getting to the top? Is the air too thin to breathe?"

"No, you can breathe everywhere here. All in all, they've set it up so if you get hurt, you are healed by sunrise. If your body is fatally wounded, we put your consciousness into a holding pattern until it's healed." He wiggled his toes as he lay on his back, and a flip-flop fell to the ground below them. Shrugging at the lost shoe, he continued, "You don't have to eat and won't be hungry. You'll have a day's energy in the morning, but if you overexert yourself, you'll get tired. So no daily marathons through the woods."

"Thanks. I guess. Why's it so hard to get to the mountaintop?"

"A boulder is attached to your ankle." Merc rose his foot. At some point the flip-flop had reappeared. "Then we set you somewhere in this world, and you begin to make your way to the top of the mountain. We let you pick the size, and the gods pick the length of the rope. So we've now come to the part where I ask you: How big of a boulder do you want?" He looked to Ferrun expectantly.

Ferrun looked down and observed the people and contemplated his inevitable fate. He could see that most of them were struggling with a rope. Most of them were stuck in place, while a few dragged it over their shoulder.

"I can pick any size I want?" Ferrun asked for clarification.

"Any size," Merc confirmed as he brushed something off his bright red Hawaiian shirt.

Ferrun didn't know much about himself, but he knew he liked puzzles and a challenge. Maybe that's what made him suitable for this Divine Trial. "Has anyone made it to the mountainside yet?"

"A few, but no one has reached the top. The ones climbing it are slow at making progress. But I'm sure they'll reach it eventually." He looked at the mountain reflectively. "Then again, maybe not. Rocks tend to get stuck at the base of the mountain more often than anywhere else."

"The rocks just get stuck?"

"Yeah, the trees and bushes get thicker near the base of the mountain. Ascension candidates get so stuck sometimes that they give up and make a home on the side of the mountain." Merc shook his head in disappointment, then looked back at Ferrun. "So what size do you want?"

A dozen possible solutions went through Ferrun's mind. He was aghast that someone would give up so easily, but he couldn't imagine the strain of dragging a rock behind him for eternity. "Is this whole thing pointless?" he asked, looking at the white-haired man.

Merc smiled a full grin this time. "Some candidates think so, but Sues and Wod both assured us that it's solvable. Someone even had Sid come in and look it over. That guy is the most compassionate towards you candidates, and he confirmed it's solvable. Although, he had doubts about how many would succeed."

Ferrun tried to imagine what dragging a small rock would feel like, then what it'd be like to carry a large rock behind him. Neither seemed like great options. Although he doubted there was an optimal-sized rock to get tied to.

"I have all the time in the world," Merc said after letting Ferrun think it over a few moments, "but I'd like to get on to the next candidate eventually."

"Tie me to the biggest rock here," Ferrun finally said. Despite the ridiculousness of the choice, it felt like a decision that suited him as comfortably as his name.

"That's an interesting start," Merc said with his now familiar grin.

Chapter Two

F errun woke up lying on hard ground. His arm buzzed with pinpricks as feeling returned to it after being squashed underneath him. He still wore the thin white linen pants and shirt from the beachfront line.

Sitting up, he saw a thicket of trees and bushes all around him. The only clearing was a steep path. A few ropes lay on the path, while others cut across it. He wasn't the first one to start down this trail.

Ferrun took a step forward to start his ascent. After a few steps there was an unexpected yank on his leg. His feet were pulled out from under him, and he fell forward, hitting his head on the ground.

Rubbing his head, he sat up and looked at his foot. A thin rope was wrapped around his ankle. Feeling the rope, he discovered it was rough and brown like an old ship's rope but only as thin as his pinky. It weighed less than he'd expected. He pulled against it to test its tensile strength, and it didn't snap despite his best efforts. His gut told him he knew a lot about the properties of various materials. He wanted to study how this thing achieved such an unlikely size, weight, and strength.

He picked at the knot around his ankle, attempting to untie it, but the knot was pulled tighter than he could undo with his fingers.

Looking around, he searched for a thin rock or stick to help him get leverage on it.

Unable to find anything nearby that would do the job, he was forced to go back into the forest. The branches and brambles of the thicket scraped his feet and ankles as he followed his rope.

Ferrun felt optimistic that he was so close to the base of the mountain. Asking for the biggest rock felt like a fitting thing to do. He hoped that being this close to the mountain was some kind of reward for his choice. Trying to focus on the positive, he hoped being held back was only a short diversion.

After several feet, he found a clearing littered with downed branches, leaves, and small rocks. He found a hardwood branch about the width of his thumb and fit it into the knot at his ankle.

Ferrun began to maneuver it, trying to get the leverage he needed to loosen the knot. He wiggled around on the rocky ground, trying to get his foot and arms in the right position. Eventually, he found a log to sit on and found an angle that gave him some promising leverage to pry against the knot.

He pulled against the stick. It was uncomfortable, but he continued to lean against the knot of the rope. The branch snapped after he put too much pressure on it. Ferrun fell off the log and onto his face.

The rocky ground scuffed his cheek, and his mouth filled with dirt and leaves. He brushed himself off and examined his sore ankle to see how far he'd gotten with the knot. Unfortunately, the rope was still as tight as when he'd started. He picked a triangle-shaped rock off the ground. Taking the same position on the log as before, he tried using the rock to untie the rope.

"Please, stop! It's hurting me to watch you," said a woman's voice.

Ferrun lost his focus and released the leverage between the rock and his knot. It was the same pressure that held him upright on the log.

He tumbled to the ground again, this time landing on his shoulder, which immediately began to throb.

"Sorry, didn't mean to startle you," the woman said.

Ferrun lifted himself off the ground, using his good shoulder, and he leaned against the fallen tree. Across the way, a young woman stepped into the clearing. She had long brown hair pulled back into a ponytail, held in place with a long root. She wore the same white linens as Ferrun. Although hers were covered in marginally less dirt than his.

"How long have you been watching?" Ferrun asked, wondering how ashamed he should be with his attempt to untie the knot.

"I heard movement in the bushes and came to see who was around. You were focused on the knot, and I wanted to see how far you would get, but your ankle is more likely to break than that rope. So I did the responsible thing and stopped you."

"Thanks, I guess." Ferrun looked down to examine the progress he'd made on the knot. The rock was shoved tightly into the knot's small gap, but the rope's hold around his ankle was just as tight.

Ferrun looked over to her ankle and found a similar knot. He looked up at her, disappointed. "I guess I should have known the knot wasn't going to come off. Thanks for stopping me before I hurt myself. I'm Ferrun." He stuck out a hand to introduce himself.

"Nice to meet you," she said, giving his hand a firm shake. "I'm Sophia." Then she unceremoniously plopped down onto the ground, sitting cross-legged. "So how big of a rock did you pick?"

Ferrun gently took a seat across from her in the clearing. His ankle was still sore from trying to untie the knot. Instead of sitting cross-legged, he stretched his leg out. "I asked for the biggest rock they had."

"You've got to be joking! Merc did explain that you're supposed to get to the top of that mountain, right?"

"Yeah, it seemed fitting at the time. I think I like a challenge."

"That's a challenge all right," she scoffed. "Well, I told them I wanted a rock the size of my hand." She held up a fist, turning it to inspect its size. "That's a reasonable size. Although in return they started me so far away from the mountain that I couldn't see it on the horizon." She stared up at the mountain poking out from behind the trees. "But now I'm here."

"I guess I'm lucky that I got put right at the base."

"Maybe, but if you can't move your rock, then you're going to have a hard time getting anywhere."

Ferrun stared at his knot, trying to think of a solution. "Do you think I could untie the rope from the rock instead?" he finally asked.

"Doubt it," Sophia answered quickly. "People don't see their rocks often. At least not me or anyone I've met. It's taken me ages to get this far, and I've met a lot of people and seen plenty of other people's rocks."

"Have you tried to untie any?"

"Hell no. If I have to drag my rock around, then they have to drag theirs. Although I have unstuck some. There's nothing more frustrating than having your rock caught somewhere you can't unstick it from."

"Is that normal around here or are you just extremely generous in helping others?" He prodded at his tender shoulder, trying to figure out how badly it was hurt.

Sophia shrugged. "It's pretty normal. I've had my rock stuck hard before and spent days tugging at it. Eventually, I went to sleep one night and woke up with it free. I gratefully moved on with the intention to pay it forward. Not that tugging on the biggest rock they've got is going to do you much good."

"Yeah," Ferrun said, deflated. "What if I went to get my rock?"

"Maybe," she said with a shrug. "I used to follow ropes when I didn't know where the mountain was. I've followed ropes for months and never seen one end or the other. Plus there's the whole problem of what you'd do with the slack. It's just infeasible."

Ferrun's back started to hurt more than his ankle, so he adjusted how he was sitting. "I don't think I have any choice. I'm going to have to find my rock and push it. I'm going to pull a muscle trying to drag it."

"Not a bad idea. You could put logs under it and move it like the Vikings moved their ships."

"The who?" Ferrun responded, confused.

"Uh, Vikings. They're..." She paused to think. "They're people who moved big ships with logs and constantly had to move the last log to the first. Memory is weird here. I have dreams of my life, but they don't all make sense together. I still have holes and gaps like this, where an idea comes, but I can't enunciate why."

"I don't remember anything from before talking with Merc, and even that's a bit cloudy."

"Yeah, that's normal."

"You think it will take me a long time to track down my boulder?"

Sophia shrugged. "Bigger rocks typically have shorter ropes. However, I didn't see it on my approach, so you're at least a few hours away."

Ferrun sighed at not being able to immediately hike up the mountain. It was so close.

"Good luck finding it. You might be the first person around here to find your rock."

"Thanks."

"You're definitely the first person dumb enough to pick a rock you can't drag," she teased.

Ferrun groaned, regretting the hubris that had gotten him into this mess. "They said there was a solution."

"They're gods. What are we going to do if they lie to us?" She stood up.

Ferrun's body ached as he got up with her. "But we're good people. We're supposed to have a chance to ascend."

"Wait for your lost memories to come back before you're so confident." She picked up the little slack of the rope that she had. "I'm glad I got to meet you, Ferrun, but I've got to get going. I want to see the first incline of the mountain before nightfall."

"Thanks for the help. I guess I'll see you around."

"I hope not. This place is big, and I plan to get out of here soon." She gestured towards the mountain. She started walking through the brambles Ferrun had come through.

Sophia disappeared into the dense forest, but her rope soon grew taut. It lifted from the ground and began jerking back and forth. It appeared that her rock was stuck on something.

"Good luck!" Ferrun called out at the top of his lungs, but if she'd heard him, she didn't respond.

Ferrun left the clearing with his rope bunched together under his arm. He was hopeful that he might find his boulder before nightfall so he could get to work devising a way to move his mistake of a rock by morning.

***

Ferrun pushed his massive ball of rope through the foot-wide gap between the trees. It wasn't an ideal path for him, but it was the one his rope unfortunately took. He'd traveled every day since he'd met Sophia but had had no luck finding his boulder. Each day, he added rope to an ever-growing ball, and after what felt like more than a month of travel, he was pushing a mass of rope bigger than him.

He took a break from trying to shove the rope through the gap to stare at the horizon. From the top of the hill, he could see the base of the mountain. The trees were thick at the base and continued up the side but eventually dwindled to nothing. As the trees thinned, the ground was white with snow and eventually merged into clouds that obscured the peak. He wondered how his body would react to the cold in the thin linens he wore.

Turning away from the mountain, he scanned the horizon for his boulder. He hoped it wouldn't be so big that he could see it above the trees, and he desperately wanted to know how much longer this wandering would last. Nothing but trees lay out in front of him, and now that his breath was calm, he got back to work forcing his ball through the opening in the trees.

The ball popped through the gap almost immediately. Ferrun didn't expect a quick success, and the mass of rope rolled down the hill. It was heavier than him and was soon dragging him by his ankle.

The ball came to rest next to a couple of trees, and Ferrun lay staring up at the blue sky, feeling every scrape and bruise on his body. He knew they would heal by dawn like his shoulder did the morning after talking to Sophia, but it would make the rest of the day's travel uncomfortable.

He soon sat up and looked around to see if anyone had noticed him. The world wasn't densely populated, but he'd run into a few more people on his short journey. Those who were tired of pulling on their rope would ask him what he was doing. Most of them had pointed out that he was going the wrong direction. He'd explain his situation to them, and everyone would respond in their own polite, or impolite, manner.

No one was around, and he decided to call it a day. It was afternoon, and he had the bruises to show he'd put in a full day's work. He unraveled some of the rope and used the slack to make a pillow and bedding, something he'd come up with after a few days of travel. It was an improvement to lying on the hard, rocky ground.

He looked up at the rope ball and figured it would be only a matter of time before it became so big that he couldn't navigate it through the forest or, worse, it would crush him. He wasn't eager to figure out what dying in the afterlife was like, so he unraveled the rope to start a second ball.

He spent the rest of the afternoon and early evening making the second ball. Ferrun hoped that his boulder was nearby. Handling one ball of rope was hard; two or more would only make things worse.

Chapter Three

When Ferrun woke up, he saw a tall man with brown skin leaning against the tree a few feet away from him. His hair was cropped short, and he was fiddling with a stick. Most of the time it fell to the ground, but occasionally it danced across his fingers. He wore the same white linens as Ferrun and had a knot around his ankle.

"Hello," Ferrun said, his sleepiness quickly fading. "Are you stuck?"

The man hadn't noticed Ferrun was awake, and the question startled him. The stick he was playing with fell to the ground out of his reach. He turned to Ferrun. "No, not yet. I was just waiting for you to wake up so I could meet you."

"Meet me? Why?"

"I've been following your rope for a while now. It led me to see the mountain and now to you. I'm Captain Isaac Teekola." He put a hand out to help Ferrun up from his bed.

"My rope goes on for a while?" Ferrun said, discouraged by the news. He let the man pull him to his feet. "Did you at least see a rock at the end of it?"

"Nah." He broke off another twig to fiddle with. "What are those things behind you?" He jabbed the new stick at the balls of rope.

Ferrun explained his situation to Teekola, including his mistake of selecting the biggest rock they had. Teekola listened while trying to get the twig to twirl around his finger. Ferrun was shocked by the interest the man took in his story. It was unlike the reactions of the others he'd met.

"I've got to say that's pretty clever," Teekola said matter-of-factly. The twig glided around his index finger and landed in the pocket between his thumb and fingers.

"You're the only one who seems to think that."

He waved the statement away with his hand. "I don't think people around here think through the problem enough."

"I surely didn't," Ferrun lamented.

"I'm a big guy, so I picked a big rock," Teekola continued. "It's heavy to pull, but I figured it's large enough to avoid areas that catch small rocks, the size I figured most people pick. It's served me well, and I think the gods went easy on me since I took on a big challenge."

"That's basically what I was thinking, but I was dumb and took it to the extreme."

"No, no, no." Teekola waved his stick back and forth like a scolding finger. "If the rock doesn't move, then it won't get stuck." He smiled a big grin and tapped his temple. "I've been wrestling with this problem lately. So far, I've freed my rope, but the forest is getting thicker, and I know eventually I will be stuck forever." He gave Ferrun a worried look.

"But at least you'll make it to the base of the mountain and can pull it up. I probably won't even be able to move mine."

"How do you know the people you've met so far aren't stuck indefinitely like you might be?" Without waiting for a response, Teekola continued, "You're onto something. If I had my rock *and* my rope, I could easily carry it to the top. I'd like to travel back along your rope with you."

Ferrun was taken aback by the faith this man put in him, a complete stranger. "You don't need my permission to do that. But I'd appreciate the company."

"Fantastic," he said with excitement, and began haphazardly picking up his rope.

"Hold on, hold on," Ferrun said, trying to keep the man from making a massive knot. "If you wrap it up like that, you won't be able to add more or unravel it if you need it. Do it like this." Ferrun showed him how to roll up the rope in a way that would be easier to manage.

It'd taken days of travel for Ferrun to figure the pattern out. He never thought he'd be teaching it to someone else. Happy to save his new friend the headache, he shared his method. Teekola caught on quickly, and soon the two set out following their parallel lines of rope.

***

Traveling through the dreary rain, Ferrun asked, "Do you remember what your life was like before this?" The question had lingered since his talk with Sophia. The two men had traveled together a few days now. They constantly exchanged ideas about how to wrap rope better and occasionally discussed the things they'd learned about this world. This was the first time they'd broached the subject of their life before this world.

Teekola didn't immediately answer the question. Instead, he messed with the new staff in his hand. He'd practically mastered spinning a twig and had moved on to spinning a stafflike branch around his wrists. He'd use it as a staff for a few steps, adding muddy rope to his ball, then take a break to spin the staff around some part of his body. It fell to the ground more often than not, and Ferrun learned to keep his distance since he didn't want a black eye or mud slung in his face. "I was the captain of a large crew." He finally answered, stabbing the staff into the ground every other step. "I spent a lot of time in space."

"Like outer space?" Ferrun said, gesturing at the cloudy sky.

"Is there another one?"

"So you lived on the moon?" Ferrun didn't find the idea of going to the moon preposterous, but living there felt advanced.

"Sure, I lived on a lot of moons, but I spent most of my time in a starship."

"How's that possible?"

"I don't really understand the engineering details, but I was in charge of making sure everyone kept things running smooth. I see it in my dreams and it feels real. When I wake up, it's a memory. It doesn't fade."

Ferrun sighed at the idea of dreams. Sophia had mentioned something similar, but despite all of his efforts, he hadn't dreamed since starting his journey to his rock. He longed for an idea of who he used to be and why he'd picked such a ridiculous challenge—a challenge he may not even deserve. Another part of him argued that even if he did dream, he probably wouldn't put much faith in them. "You sure you aren't just imagining that spaceship?"

"Starship," Teekola corrected him. "I was a captain and led a crew of a thousand or so people. We did vacation transport between a few different star systems."

"Like a cruise ship?" Ferrun didn't know where the words came from, and it reminded him of Sophia's Viking comment. Talking to Teekola about dreams seemed to help his memory. It was uncomfortable drudging up muddy knowledge he didn't remember putting there.

"That's an archaic way to put it. We didn't move resources or run military ships. Just dealt with people. Not that they weren't a handful sometimes."

"And you're sure you didn't just dream all this up?" Ferrun knew getting to the moon was a challenge and that it was debated if traveling to a different star system was even possible.

"It's real. I remember that we had a chef with a kid who didn't want to eat what the mess hall served, and it caused a whole fiasco. I remember half the handbook I studied at the flight academy and can cite a few regulations. I know the key code to my captain's quarters was D504. Why would I make up all those scattered memories?"

"I guess you wouldn't."

"No kidding I wouldn't." He swung the staff over his wrist twice. The second time, it flung wide and flew past Ferrun's head. The handle landed in a puddle, and the tip was pointed at Ferrun.

"You think I'll get my memories back like you?" Ferrun picked up his pace to get ahead of Teekola.

"Don't see why you wouldn't." The sucking sound of mud followed every step the Captain took towards the staff.

"What if I'm a bad person?"

"Maybe you are. Sometimes I dream that my starship crashed because of a mistake I made. Or it had a malfunction I should have caught, and we got stranded between stars and starved to death. Maybe that's how I died."

"You think these gods would let us do this trial if we were bad people?"

"Maybe that's why we got the trial." Teekola swung the wet stick around his wrists as he kept walking. Ferrun kept a quick pace to stay ahead of the man's long strides and avoid getting hit. "The only higher powers I ever engaged with were the bureaucrats who designed my routes. I don't know why the gods chose me as an ascension candidate. They were always myths in my mind."

Ferrun soon changed the subject back to knots to avoid the uncomfortable questions that filled his mind like the rain filled their footprints.

Chapter Four

The pair got to know each other better as the weeks of travel passed. Ferrun still had knowledge pop into his head as he talked to Teekola but didn't have dreams so vivid that they stood out as memories. He knew firmly that he'd never experienced space travel—only a few people had in his time period. He lived on a planet named Earth, and it was a place Teekola's society had left countless generations ago.

Ferrun walked with a limp that day. He'd stepped on a sharp stick with his heel that morning. The pair discussed the inconvenience of having to walk barefoot while traveling at a slower pace.

"It'll be fixed in the morning," Teekola said.

"I know. I just would have appreciated a pair of shoes if I'm supposed to spend my afterlife hiking around."

"You don't think shoes are insulting to the gods? Besides, all the shoes I've ever worn were maybe a few millimeters thick. They were just polite fashion on the ship."

"How are shoes insulting?"

Instead of hearing the Captain's response, Ferrun heard cursing farther into the forest. Interested in meeting someone else, the pair agreed to let out some slack to investigate. After only a few feet, a man was visible through the trees. He was tugging at his rope.

"How's it going?" Teekola said as the pair approached.

"I've made it maybe three feet today," the man said, "and I don't even know if I'm going in the right direction."

Teekola stretched out a large hand. "I'm Captain Isaac Teekola, and this is Ferrun. You're headed in the right direction."

"I'm Gaellen." He shook his hand. "How do you know where the mountain is?"

"We lost sight of it only a few days ago," Ferrun replied, pulling his newest ball of rope nearby to sit on.

"What's that?" Gaellen said.

"Rope." Teekola leaned on his staff. "We've been collecting it. That's how we know where the mountain is."

"You saw the mountain and didn't head towards it?"

"I'm not able to drag my boulder," Ferrun said.

"Yeah, that's why you keep pulling on it." Gaellen made a half-hearted tug on his rope.

Ferrun then explained that he'd asked for the largest boulder the gods had.

"And what's your excuse, *Captain*?" The last word came out teasingly instead of reverently, and Ferrun didn't appreciate it.

"I liked his plan of going back to his rock," Teekola said, balancing his staff on the edge of his hand.

Gaellen scoffed. "You're taking the advice of someone who, after being told the goal was to hike up a mountain, picked an immovable rock. I'm not sure which one of you is the bigger fool."

Ferrun thought the man made a good point.

"It makes sense though," Teekola said. "Just think. You could be navigating your rock around obstacles now instead of pulling it behind you."

"After, what, three, maybe four months of picking up my rope?"

Teekola shrugged. "You have an eternity."

"I want to make it up that mountain as fast as possible, so I'm going to do it the way God intended." Gaellen picked up his rope and began tugging on it with even more vigor.

Teekola began making some other comments in Ferrun's defense, but Ferrun didn't know if they were to protect Teekola's ego or Ferrun's plan.

As if to counter all of Teekola's points, Gaellen's rope lurched free as the rock broke through whatever obstacle had held it back. Gaellen said goodbye and walked away from the two men and their balls of rope.

Teekola began letting out slack to follow him, but Ferrun placed a hand on his shoulder to stop him. "You know he's not going to change his mind."

"Yeah. He's got the better part of eternity to come to his senses." Teekola began wrapping up the slack he'd let out.

***

Ferrun and Teekola sat on their rope balls, leaning against a tree. The moon was full, and Ferrun wondered if this was the second or third full moon he'd seen. Teekola played with a stick he'd found and was trying to get it to jump between his hands with a twirl. They hadn't met anyone in the weeks since they'd found Gaellen, but the interaction was still on Ferrun's mind.

"I used to be able to do this with a stylus," Teekola said, peering at the stick. "But my muscles just don't remember."

"What if Gaellen's right?" Ferrun asked.

"That guy knows about as much as a rookie navigator."

"We don't know anything about this world. Merc made it sound like this place is an infinite plane, and I might be sending you on a three-year journey to find your rock."

"I had to take a few math classes to become a captain. Three years is less than infinity."

"But if it's a race, then someone might beat you to the top."

"You know how they invented the jump drive we used?"

"I barely understand the engines we used to get to the moon."

"I don't understand the details either. I just needed to know a little bit about a lot of things. I know they figured it out by not following the traditional understanding of physics. They couldn't brute-force their way past the speed of light, so they took another approach."

"But I'm not some genius physicist." Ferrun still didn't know what he was. "I earned a lot of degrees, and I've done some research and published papers, but I didn't make any waves with it."

"Maybe you were saving all your good ideas for the afterlife." The twig in Teekola's hand successfully leapt from one hand to the other. In the dim light of the moon, it looked like the twig had a will of its own.

"If picking the biggest boulder is my best idea, I'm not sure I'm cut out for this Divine Trial."

Teekola laid out his rope like a bed and said, "I don't know you well enough to know why you picked an impossible challenge. I don't think you do either. Luckily, you've got an eternity to figure it out."

"What if I don't figure it out by then?"

"I don't think you've wrapped your head around the idea of eternity, friend." He lay down to go to sleep.

Ferrun messed with his rope, trying to untie the knot at his ankle even though he knew it was useless. He eventually gave up on the endeavor. Tired from a long day of walking, he stretched himself out on a rope bed of his own.

***

Ferrun stood on the corner of the street. It was the same corner where he always waited for his bus. He listened to a podcast, but the words weren't clear to him. He had a satchel full of research papers slung over his shoulder, and he wondered how he was going to explain being this late to work.

A little girl, maybe six or seven, distracted him by bouncing a ball up and down. She should have been at her school; he should have been at his school too. The past week had dragged on, and today didn't promise to be any better. Ferrun was just as capable of not making progress in his apartment as in his office. And not making progress seemed like the only thing he could do lately.

The little girl played with one of those overinflated plastic balls that bounced further than expected. As a kid, he'd always beg his father to buy him one, but his dad always said they had plenty of toys at home. As an adult, he realized it was likely because his dad couldn't stand the incessant *boing* sound it made every time it bounced.

Ferrun watched the bus turn the corner and head towards the crowded stop. Just about everyone at the bus stop saw it. He got his bus pass ready as others got up off the benches. The only person who didn't notice was the girl. She was having fun with her ball, bouncing it as hard as she could.

The air brakes of the bus engaged, letting out a hiss that echoed down the street. People crowded around the area where the first door would stop when the bus eventually arrived. Ferrun always waited for the second door so he could peacefully sit in the back. He'd found a chip in the sidewalk months ago and used it to gauge the right place to stand.

The driver was new, an older man with wavy white hair and an equally white beard. That might have been the reason the bus was late, but a few minutes weren't going to make a difference to Ferrun's tardiness.

An ad for some sort of cereal Ferrun would never try played in his ear as he watched the bus approach. He saw the driver's face change first, then the wheels on the bus began to screech as rubber melted to the pavement. The harsh smell of burnt rubber filled the air.

Ferrun looked to where the bus was headed and saw the girl. Her blue dress flowed behind her as a white shoe fell off her foot. They weren't made for the running she was doing. She was probably dressed up to go somewhere nice, nicer than the claustrophobic office where Ferrun would spend his afternoon. He would read more material science papers, looking for a different approach to his problem. One that might yield results.

The girl chased her ball into the street. The ball was headed towards the median, and the girl, like a cloud in the wind, followed it off the curb.

She was almost within arm's reach of Ferrun. He could take a step, maybe two, and grab her out of the bus's path, but his body was frozen in that strange way that only dream bodies could be frozen. A woman called out the name of the girl: Ally, or Amy, or Anny. It wasn't clear in the chaos.

Startled by the sound of the bus, the girl realized her mistake and the excitement of chasing her ball was replaced with terror. The front of the bus blocked Ferrun's view of the girl, who probably never fully understood her mistake. He was standing too far behind the front of the bus to see the horror the rest of the crowd saw.

He pushed against the paralysis that held him back from making his way towards the crowd. There had to be something he could do to help. Unfortunately, the time for him to help had passed. His foot broke free from the paralysis. When it landed on the ground, it jolted him awake.

***

Ferrun sat up on his bed of rope. He'd finally had a dream like Teekola described. It wasn't fading away, but that only made him feel more ashamed that he hadn't done anything to help the girl. He was grateful some of his past had finally returned to him, but if his life was full of horrors like that, he didn't know how much more he wanted to remember.

Chapter Five

In the morning, Ferrun started his third ball of rope. They were averaging about one ball every time the moon turned. The pair often discussed whether this world was paradise. Teekola was happy with his lot considering he'd never expected a life after death. However, Ferrun didn't think this world was what he'd imagined. He was willing to concede that while it wasn't paradise, he suspected it had a lot of things going for it.

The pair passed more people like Gaellen as they got closer to the edge of the forest. Teekola, always willing to use as much of eternity as possible, took time to let out slack and chat with them.

Some people shared their theories about the world. A few talked about how they were in the outermost circle of hell based on some holy text they remembered. Ferrun's memory was slowly coming back to him, and the fact that the details of these books were vague made him figure he never took religion too seriously in his life. A few people were eager to point out that this was likely the reason he was here, and he didn't have enough evidence to prove them wrong.

Teekola was always eager to share Ferrun's rock idea with anyone they met. Despite this, they hadn't found any takers.

"If they're not going to listen to us, then why talk about it with them?" Ferrun asked as he coiled his rope. The evening was cool, and the sun was beginning to set.

"It's the right thing to do." Teekola scooped some rope up with his walking stick.

"It's making us look like fools more than anything else." He looked up to make sure he wasn't going to walk into anything and saw something strange hanging from a tree branch.

"I know you don't love their reactions, but they might use the information someday. Plus, you may never—"

"That's a person," Ferrun said in shock.

"Exactly, they're all people, and we need to do what we can to help them."

Ferrun began running towards the man in the tree. Teekola, taken aback by the reaction, finally looked up.

"Have you ever seen a dead person in this world?" Ferrun asked, looking up at the man hanging in the tree.

"I didn't even know you could die in the afterlife," Teekola said once he'd joined Ferrun. He poked the body with his staff, and it swung back and forth.

Ferrun could follow the rope from the man's ankle up the tree, around the branch, and looped around the man's neck. His face was purple, and the rest of the body was drained of color. The man hadn't been hanging there long enough to start decomposing, and Ferrun was grateful for that.

"Let's at least bury him," Ferrun suggested.

"How?" Teekola said. By his tone Ferrun could tell he was eager to move along.

Ferrun searched the ground and found a flat stone that he could use as a shovel. "With this."

"How do you want to get him down? We can't just cut the rope. Let's just hike a little bit further and make camp for the night."

"I'm not going to be able to sleep with a body looming behind us. We should at least save the next traveler from having to find it. You're always wanting to help people. Why not help this guy?"

Teekola sighed. "If he hanged himself, he didn't think there was any hope left."

Without trying to drag further agreement out of Teekola, Ferrun climbed up the tree using a little bit of his slack. He quickly uncovered why the man had likely done it: There was no slack in his rope. Teekola was probably right; the man's rock was likely stuck somewhere and he simply gave up.

Ferrun pulled at the noose around the man's neck, but that wasn't helping. Pulling the body up by the line wouldn't loosen the knot. Additionally, since there was no slack in the rope, there was no way to lower the body.

"Can you lift his feet to give me some slack?" Ferrun asked.

Teekola mashed a ball of rope flat enough to stand on and used it as a stool. He hefted the dead man's legs onto his shoulders, and Ferrun was able to slip the noose off his neck.

By the time Ferrun got down from the tree, Teekola had laid the man at the base of the tree. Ferrun got to work digging a hole while Teekola poked around for a similar rock to help with.

Digging the hole was a slow process. The light of the day was fading, they were exhausted from the day's travels, and they didn't have the right tools. When they had gotten a fair way into the hole, Ferrun heard a rustling behind him. His mind expected to see a predator, but there were no animals in this world. He turned on his heels to face the strange sound.

The formerly hanged man sat up, and his face was regaining its natural color. "Not again," the man said with a hoarse voice. He brushed dirt off his white linens. The faint moonlight showed dark purple bruises around his neck.

Ferrun jumped in place and held the dirt-covered stone out in front of him, partly in defense and partly as a peace offering. As he did this his back foot slipped into the grave and he lost his balance, falling to the ground clumsily.

"Relax," the man said in a less raspy voice. He started massaging his bruised neck and got up from the ground.

Ferrun was flailing in the hole and quickly realized that it was neither deep enough nor long enough for him or any grown man to lie in.

"I had a bad feeling about messing with this," Teekola said, then offered Ferrun a hand to help lift him out.

"You were"—Ferrun gestured at the man and then the limb where they'd found him—"dead."

The man leaned against the same tree he had hung from. "Only as dead as they'll let me be. You can't really die round here. If you haven't tried it out yet, then I'm happy to inform you of this dreadful news."

Teekola pulled up a rope ball and sat on it, dusting the dirt off his knees.

"But you were dead," Ferrun said.

"I was unconscious; my mind was somewhere else." The man looked past Ferrun longingly. "But once I was no longer suffocating, my body came back to life." He made a gesture at his current state. "I'm sure you thought you were doing me a favor taking me down and all, but now I have to go through the work of getting myself back up there." He looked up at the branch as if staring up at a lover in a castle tower.

"Sorry?" Teekola apologized.

"Nah, it's fine," he said, cracking a grin. "Every once in a while, someone will do it. Usually, they break my ankles getting me down, and that hurts like hell. So thanks for being gentle with me." He nodded to Teekola, correctly guessing who'd lowered him down.

The man then saw what Teekola was sitting on. His eyes went wide at the sight of all the rope. "Those belong to you two?"

"Yeah, they're attached to our rocks," Teekola said, patting his seat.

The previously dead man approached the balls of rope. He looked at them like an addict about to get his fix. He reached out to feel them, but the rope at his ankle stopped him short. The tug pulled him out of his trance, and he looked up at Teekola. "How did you get that much slack? You'll be at the mountain in no time. Maybe even halfway up it."

"It's exactly enough to get him to the base of the mountain," Teekola responded on Ferrun's behalf.

The man's eyes went wide. "Why the hell are you wasting your time here with me? You know how long it's been since I've had slack?" He didn't wait for a response. "Years. You know how I know it's been years?" He barreled through any chance the pair had to reply. "Because every morning I wake up at sunrise, conscious and able to breathe. Then I choke to death from the rope."

Teekola cursed, and his tone was a mix of amazement and fear.

"Before that," the man continued, "I was stuck here tugging against my rope. I don't know what it's stuck on, but it isn't coming free, and no one else has freed it yet." He gave it a hard tug for emphasis. "For all I know, it's looped round a tree branch of its own." He kicked his leg again, tugging lightly at the rope. "I pulled on it for years and I kept pulling. I refused to give up. I thought that was the key—never give up."

"That seems like a good idea," Ferrun said, forcing the interjection.

"Then one day I finally started wondering what the point of it all was," the man continued. "A few weeks later I decided I might as well try being dead for a bit." He chuckled at this last statement. "Best decision I ever made."

"How's that?" Teekola said, sounding dubious.

The man sank back against the tree as he answered. "The memories and dreams usually make it worth it. I get to experience my life again."

"It was that good?" Ferrun said.

"Not particularly. I had a family though. I saw them occasionally when I wasn't away on business. I get to see them again...in my dreams."

Teekola let out a hum of agreement, and Ferrun wondered if he had a family; he hadn't remembered them yet.

The man began fiddling with his rope. "I was a salesman. Traveled a lot. Sold steel to factories in the Midwest. It paid okay, but I wanted more. That's what causes the nightmares."

"Why die if it gives you nightmares?" Ferrun asked.

"Because it's better than the nothing I feel here. I committed arson," he said, almost ashamed, "and it was just my luck that the fire spread too quickly for me to get out of the factory." He let out a sigh. "Sometimes I make it out, but in those dreams my kids are stuck inside."

"You burned a building down with your kids inside?" Teekola asked. His hand was clutched in a fist around his staff.

The man shook his head, but it wasn't full of conviction. "I don't think so. I think it's just part of how this world haunts me. Soon enough I'm alive again, eating a Christmas dinner with them or watching them play in the park with the Labrador."

"Why'd you commit arson?" Ferrun asked.

"The factory owner, a customer of mine, said they'd cut me in on the insurance money. I figured I could take it and spend more time with my family instead of having to travel so much."

"Doesn't sound like that worked out," Teekola said.

"Things went from bad to worse," the man said as he crouched to yank on the rope. It pulled tight and then he let it fall limp as he stood up.

"Have you ever considered following your rope to find your rock?" Ferrun was surprised Teekola hadn't brought up the idea yet.

"Before today? No. Seeing you two, I considered it, but it's not worth it. You're moving away from the goal. While I'm not getting closer to the mountain like some, at least I'm not losing ground like you." He threw his rope over the branch and tugged at it to make sure it would hold his weight once again.

"Eventually you'll head towards it again," Ferrun pointed out.

The man shrugged. "This world is against us. It's an empty and lifeless place, and if I'm not caught on this obstacle, I'll get caught on the next. I always wanted more in life. Maybe that's what I'm here to learn. Giving up means I stop playing the game, stop wanting to win and just enjoy my family like I didn't get to in life." He grabbed at the lower branches and started hoisting himself up the tree.

Ferrun tried to think of something he could say to convince the man not to hang himself again. All that came to mind was, "If I see your rock, I'll try to free it up."

"Thanks, kid." The man climbed up to his branch. "But don't worry too much about it. I probably wouldn't use the slack. I like this tree—sturdy branches."

Ferrun frowned and looked up at the man perched on the tree branch, not knowing what to say.

The hanged man did him a favor and broke the silence. "If you two don't mind moving on, I have some stuff to take care of." He made a dusting motion with his finger to shoo the two away from his tree.

Teekola didn't need any encouragement, but Ferrun's eyes lingered. The last thing he saw before pulling his gaze away was the man crowning himself with the noose.

***

"I just can't believe someone would do that," Teekola said. A week had passed since they'd parted from the hanged man, but it was a topic they often found themselves coming back to.

"He's just working with what he's got." Ferrun found himself taking the man's side more often than not.

"He should push for more instead of giving up and not doing anything. The dreams of his death and life have become his world."

"His rock's stuck. I'm eventually going to get to where he is. I'll be standing next to my rock, and maybe if I'm lucky, it will be tall enough to hang myself from." It was a dark thought that lurked on the edge of his mind.

"But you'll keep working at it. If you put in hard work, you'll find success."

"How do you put hard work into a boulder too heavy to move?"

"You'll figure it out eventually."

"Will I? That guy put in hard work pulling against his rock, but it didn't get him anywhere."

"But we came along with an alternate solution for him."

"And what? You think someone else with a massive immovable rock will just come wandering by me and give me another point of view?" Ferrun picked up his rope, looping it around his arm faster.

"I don't know how to convince you it will be okay."

"Because you don't know it will be okay. You're trusting some cruel deities that tied us all up. I wish they'd just recycled my consciousness like normal."

"I've heard of worse afterlives," Teekola said.

Ferrun wasn't interested in exploring alternative tortures. This one was bad enough. They spent the rest of the day on simpler conversations and silence. Ferrun mulled over the scenario of the hanged man through the silence and through that evening. Even as he fell asleep, he wondered what would differentiate his fate from the fate of the hanged man.

Chapter Six

F errun stood on the curb and watched the girl bounce the ball. He wasn't interested in the bus or the driver. He knew what was going to happen and wanted to do everything he could to stop it.

Unfortunately, he was once again paralyzed in a standing position. The fumes of the bus got closer, and he heard it begin to slow down. He knew it wouldn't slow down fast enough.

He watched the girl follow the ball into the street. He fought the feeling of being locked into place. He freed himself and took a step towards the girl.

He tugged at her dress. She weighed more than he expected. He had expected her to fly back with a light tug. She fought him, not realizing how he was helping.

Something hit his shoulder and he was pushed back. He fell onto the curb, and the front wheels of the bus crushed his leg. His head hit the concrete. People screamed in panic all around him. Darkness faded in from the edges of his vision.

***

He woke up in a hospital bed. His leg was bandaged along with most of his torso and left arm. His right arm was taped up with various tubes coming out of it.

He saw a man sitting in the corner, tapping a pencil on a book of crossword puzzles.

"Dad?" Ferrun asked. He hadn't known who the man was, but now he wondered how he could ever forget him. His father had thin gray hair that lay long across his scalp, and rare stubble covered his cheeks and chin, an unusual look for the man.

"Grazie a Dio," he said, putting his book down. "You're an idiot for getting hurt like this."

Ferrun didn't think he could disagree.

"But I'm glad you're okay."

"The girl?" Ferrun asked.

"She didn't make it." His father looked at the floor.

"How long until I'm able to get back to work?"

"I'm going to take care of you for at least a few months."

"You can't do that." The protest out of politeness morphed into doubt in his father's ability to take care of himself let alone his injured son.

"I raised you for eighteen years." The comment was paired with a hand that waved away Ferrun's protest.

Vague memories argued that the number was definitely on the higher side of accurate, but back then there was a lot going on in both of their lives.

"Your brother is in another state, and your sisters have kids of their own to take care of." He pressed a call button while they argued about how Ferrun would recover.

Soon a nurse came in wearing tattered brown scrubs just this side of being wearable. His hair was curled in tight circles near his scalp. His name tag, which hung from a marigold-orange lanyard, said his name was simply Sidd.

"Take a nap," Sidd said. "You won't be leaving here anytime soon, so just rest." His voice was compassionate and comfortable and felt like something perfected over countless lifetimes.

"I'll get it worked out," his father said reassuringly. "Just rest."

Ferrun wanted to fight with his father more, wanted to assure the man he wouldn't have to be burdened by his son's failed heroics, but his eyelids were heavy, and he couldn't keep them open any longer.

***

Ferrun kept an eye on his steps as he followed Teekola through the thinning trees of the forest. He collected rope methodically, and the man in front of him was moving faster than Ferrun could keep up with.

Since waking up, he'd felt bad about not trusting his father. When he was younger, he had respected the man, but time and his father's actions had eroded that. Ferrun wondered if not trusting his father made him a bad person.

"How'd I get better at this than you?" Teekola called back. He'd taken a break by leaning against his walking stick.

"I want it to be done right." The answer was only half true.

"When was the last time we saw the mountain?" Teekola asked. "Maybe a month ago, right?"

"At least two," Ferrun said, weaving the rope into its ball shape.

Teekola sucked on his teeth in a hissing sound. He was spinning his staff and getting quite good at it. He rarely dropped it now. Whenever it did fall to the ground, he could kick it back up into his hands.

"Why do you ask?" Ferrun was now standing near the man but kept some distance to avoid getting whacked.

"The ball doesn't have to be perfect," Teekola said, catching the stick in his hand and jabbing it towards Ferrun's newest and neatest rope ball.

Ferrun looked at the ball Teekola had started, and it looked just this side of tangled. "Unlike you, I'm going to be stuck with this for a while. So it needs to be done right."

"Oh, come on." The man let a toothy grin crawl across his face. "When you get to your rock, you can retie it so it's neater. Not like you'll have anything else to do." Teekola grinned as the staff twirled in front of his body.

Ferrun groaned at the insinuation and continued to slowly pick up the slack. Behind him he heard Teekola's staff sweep through the air a few more times. Once there were a few yards between them, he heard the crunch of leaves under Teekola's feet.

"You think starships are perfect?" Teekola asked once he'd caught up.

Ferrun shrugged.

"They're not. Far from it. They're always a hair above passing inspection, and we trust them to take us through the vacuum of space."

"Seems risky."

"It probably is, but it could be worse. We could be stuck on a single planet or single star system. We'd never experience the benefits of other worlds."

"This is the only non-Earth planet I've experienced, and I'm not even sure it's a planet."

"But we never told the passengers that we skirted past inspections. We never even told the rest of the crew. Sure, engineering knew they had some parts assembled in nontraditional ways. The cook knew he had only a few days of extra rations if the trip ran long. The custodial crew knew the nooks of the ship that hadn't been cleaned in weeks because they didn't have the staff. However, I was the only one who knew how close the ship was to the edge."

"I don't exactly have the luxury of separating my brain from my body," Ferrun said.

"I didn't get flustered. I couldn't." Teekola stuck his stick into the ground for emphasis. "If I had let it get to me, everyone would see through the mirage in a heartbeat. I got calls from every department all day long. Listening to problems was my job. Then I'd prioritize them and enable the crew to fix the crucial ones."

"I don't have a shortage of problems."

"Exactly, but you've got to trust yourself to solve them. Just like I trusted my crew to solve them."

"And if they couldn't solve the problem?"

"Then I'd call in a tug ship to get us out of the mess. Or we'd die and then it wouldn't be my problem anymore."

"Is that how you died?"

"I don't think so. I think I was a good captain, but this isn't about captaining."

"No kidding."

"You'll figure it out," Teekola said. He'd stopped to spin his staff. "I trust you like I trusted my crew. Captains can't know everything, but we get a good sense of who to trust with our lives. You're worth trusting. I knew that day one. And I trust you'll get your massive rock moving when you get there. Maybe you'll have to build an apparatus to move your damn boulder, but I know you'll figure it out."

Ferrun stopped gathering rope since Teekola had stopped following him. "It's just past midday. We can't call it quits this early."

Teekola gestured perpendicular to Ferrun's path with his staff. "My rope goes that way now."

Ferrun looked down to his feet, and sure enough there wasn't the familiar parallel rope. "I guess we have all of eternity. We can call it early today."

Teekola told more stories about the planets he'd visited and the technology he'd used. Most of it sounded like science fiction to Ferrun, but he was entertained by the idea that humanity had made it to the stars and beyond in some far future.

They woke up the next morning well rested as always, and after the awkward silence spent rolling up their beds of rope, Teekola spoke. "I've known this day was coming for a long time. We passed landmarks that remind me of when I first found your rope. I'm sorry I have to leave you."

"I've appreciated the company," Ferrun said, fighting back something that was caught in his throat. "I hope you find your rock soon." Teekola was the first close friend he'd made in this world, and maybe his last based on how people reacted to his ideas.

"Same for you. I'm sure it's close by."

Ferrun had a melancholy smile. "If you make it to the top before me, leave a note or something. I'll make sure to do the same." There was no way Ferrun would ever catch up with his immovable rock. Once he found his boulder, he would have to conquer the unfathomable task of maneuvering the heavy thing up the mountain.

"You showed me a new way to live in this world, and it's far more relaxing than constantly fighting with my rock," Teekola said. "I appreciate you, and I will share your teachings with whoever I meet. Regardless of how they take it."

"I don't know if I could have kept going without your encouragement. You helped me try new ways of wrapping my rope, and the worlds you've seen are fascinating. I'll keep your optimism in mind."

"You're about to need a fourth ball, friend," Teekola said with a wide smile. "I hope you find your rock sooner rather than later. Otherwise, the boulder will look small compared to the ropes you're carrying."

Ferrun laughed as they hugged. Once the man's long arms let go, they parted ways.

The following days were filled with loneliness. Ferrun had no one to discuss ideas or share stories with. Talking during his travels had helped him pass the time, and he wondered if anyone would ever be as willing and excited to pick up their rope as Teekola had been.

II

Ocean

Chapter Seven

The farther from the mountain Ferrun traveled, the more people he passed. However, each of them moved along quickly. Few travelers got stuck this far from the mountain. Those who did get stuck could free themselves after only a few tugs.

After Ferrun explained to them why he had so much rope, the travelers would berate him for the decision. They always asked, "Do you know which direction the mountain is?"

The fewer the problems people had with their own rocks, the sillier his plan to find his rock seemed—to all parties involved. He wondered why the gods tortured him and why he continued to participate.

Day after day, Ferrun collected his rope slowly and meditatively as the old balls of slack rolled behind him like pool balls lined up for the perfect shot. He was worried about how long the rope was. Larger rocks usually meant shorter ropes, according to Merc and other travelers, but by that logic, he should have found his boulder by now. Something had made the gods change their strategy, and that wasn't comforting.

His number of rope balls soon entered the teens. The only positive thing he could think of with them behind him was that he wouldn't have to use logs to roll his boulder around as Sophia had initially suggested. He had enough slack that the rope itself could work as a rolling mechanism.

Unfortunately, as his rope balls piled up, so did his problems. He had so much rope that he didn't know if he'd be able to navigate it through the thickets at the base of the mountain. His boulder probably wouldn't navigate that area well either. With each day of travel, his mind found new problems to dwell on.

At night he tried to sketch out solutions in the dirt or imagine how to tackle the challenges. Unfortunately, they were complex, and he didn't truly believe he could pull them off. The biggest problem was moving the boulder in the first place, followed by moving it up the steep sides of the mountain.

One day Ferrun walked from the shade of the trees into a clearing. The dirt under his toes felt soft. He looked up to see it turn into sand and eventually water.

He followed his rope with his eyes and found that it went into the water. Deflated, he made his way to the water's edge and didn't bother coiling up the slack. Once he reached the water, he bent over to taste it.

As soon as it hit his lips, he spat it out. He stood at the edge of an ocean. The realization filled his heart with dread.

He looked at his collection of rope balls covered in sand from rolling along the beach. An idea popped into his mind. He had to test it and didn't know what he'd do if it didn't work out.

He pushed his newest ball into the ocean, wading in up to his knees behind it. The ball rolled on the sandy floor the entire way. He pulled the ball back to the shore and lay down in the sand, defeated.

The sky was clear blue, but a storm of frustration brewed in Ferrun's mind. His rope balls didn't float. It'd be impossible to swim across the ocean with them attached to him like anchors.

The sun beat down on him, and soon his brow was covered in sweat. He dragged himself out of the sun and under the shade of a tree to cool down. He looked at the expanse of the ocean and the endless shore headed off in both directions. There were no shells, but driftwood, seaweed, and rocks littered the beach.

He heard something splashing in the water. The sound made it easy to find the person swimming towards the shore.

He walked towards the person to make sure they were okay. It was a woman dragging a smooth log out of the water. She plopped it down once she was clear of the waves. In exhaustion she dropped herself to the sand and leaned against the log. As Ferrun approached he shouted a greeting from across the beach.

"Hey," she said, and gave Ferrun a small wave that looked like it took all the energy she had left.

Once he got close enough to speak without shouting, he could hear her heavy breathing. Her white, nearly transparent linens clung to her body. "How far did you swim?" he asked, averting his gaze from her. He looked out across the waves.

"The whole thing," she said, starting to catch her breath.

"Really?" Ferrun looked at her in shock, trying to gauge if she were serious.

"Yeah," the response came as if it were the only reasonable answer. "My rope led away from the shore, so I figured swimming across was the way to go."

Ferrun couldn't believe his ears. He stared at her in shock, then realized that might make her uncomfortable, so he looked back to the ocean. "How long did that take?"

"I don't know," she answered with a sigh. "It felt like forever. There wasn't a mountain on that side of the ocean. My rope led away from the beach, so that seemed like an omen to cross it." She stood up and looked out to sea with Ferrun. "You're the first human I've seen in all my time in this world."

Ferrun thought about it. "Yeah, I guess I would be." He had been passing people on a regular basis, but it was only because he was going against the flow.

"What are you looking at?" she asked.

"Nothing. It's just that..." Ferrun didn't know how to politely put the situation into words. "Your clothes are wet." He gestured at her shirt.

"Yeah, of course they're wet. I just got out of the—" She looked down and laughed. "What? You've never seen breasts before?"

"I have," he blurted, adding, "I think I have. I just thought—"

She cut him off. "Doesn't bother me." Reaching out her hand, she said, "I'm Gesa."

"Nice to meet you. I'm Ferrun." He then changed the subject back to something he was comfortable with. "You're definitely heading in the right direction." Counting up the balls he had stored in the shade, he added, "It's going to be over a year's walk at least."

"That's fine. At least I won't have to hold onto a log the whole time and worry about drowning," she said with a laugh.

Ferrun shuddered at the idea, then realized he was about to have to face the same thing. "I can't believe you did that, and now I have to do it."

"Why would you do that?"

"I have to get all these balls of rope across the ocean." He gestured at the balls he had left sitting under a tree.

"That's all slack?! How in the world did you wind up with that much slack?"

Ferrun explained why he had the balls of rope and why he was walking towards his rock instead of up the mountain.

When he was finished, Gesa's clothes were dry, and they were both leaning against the log.

"You're going to need a boat," she said. "No idea how you're going to build one though. I tried but couldn't find a way to hold the logs together. Then I remembered Merc said we were effectively immortal here, so I decided to swim across."

"I have enough rope to tie the logs together."

"Probably a few times over. Can I see them?" She got up before he responded.

"Sure," he said, unsure of what was interesting about the balls of rope.

The two got up and walked away from the shore. They made it only a few steps before Gesa's rope went taut and she couldn't move any farther. She bent over, picked it up, and tugged at it.

"Son of a swine!" she cursed. "It's stuck. Hold on." She tugged at it some more. Gesa buried her feet in the sand to get traction.

After she tried a bit without much success, Ferrun lent her a hand. The two of them pulled at the rope without making any progress until the backs of their shirts were dripping with sweat.

Gesa threw down the rope and fell back into the sand in frustration. She tugged lightly on the rope by moving her foot, unwilling to give in.

"We'll try again in a bit. I'm sure we'll get it unstuck soon," Ferrun said, attempting to cheer her up.

Soon they'd caught their breath and tried again. After only a few minutes, Gesa gave up and once again plopped herself down into the sand. "It's pointless. It's stuck at the bottom of the sea."

"Maybe it's just caught on a tree or root. Someone might free it."

"There's nothing on that side of the ocean. The trees are thin, and beyond that is desert. There's nothing for a rock to get caught on. It's got to be stuck at the bottom of the ocean. No one is going to pass it to free it." She looked away from the water. "I can't even make it to the shade of those trees, let alone the mountain. I'm going to be stuck on this beach in the sun for the rest of eternity."

Seeing how upset she was, Ferrun added, "I could bring you some leaves to make some shade for you."

"Shade isn't my real problem," Gesa scoffed.

"Yeah, I guess not." Ferrun looked from her ankle to the wet sandy rope that came out of the ocean only a few yards away.

"I guess you're going to be getting some help with that boat," Gesa said. "If you want it."

Ferrun beamed with excitement. "Thank God. There was no way I was going to be able to do it myself."

They spent the rest of the afternoon drawing out design ideas in the sand. Gesa had a lot of knowledge about how to build seafaring boats out of rudimentary supplies but didn't go into why. Ferrun was just grateful that he might wind up on something that didn't immediately sink.

Once dusk came, Ferrun brought his balls of rope to the shore and built a bed for Gesa and another for himself. He fell asleep remembering how pleasant it was to have someone traveling with him.

***

Ferrun sat on the edge of the barstool, leaning forward so his feet were on the floor instead of the footrest. "I can't believe I did it."

"Me neither," the man next to him said.

Ferrun looked over and saw the long face of Jeremy, his best friend since he started his master's a decade ago. His face was framed with his long black hair that he occasionally had pulled into a ponytail or bun.

"But I'm glad you did," Jeremy continued, "you're better off pursuing something else."

"They're going to fire me." Ferrun's chest sank.

"They were going to fire you if you stayed with that project. You weren't publishing anything."

"But I could have published something great if I'd stuck with it," Ferrun groaned. His funding had come from a construction company looking for more efficient structural materials, but their tolerances were ambitious to say the least. The company was tight-lipped about what they needed it for, and Ferrun was one of the few willing to apply for the grant money.

"Maybe," Jeremy said, then took a sip of his beer. There wasn't anything that could reassure Ferrun right now, and his friend knew it.

"It seemed so promising," Ferrun continued. Today he'd officially given up pursuing the project after five years of work. He'd chosen not to reapply for the grant and would move on to another project even though every other open project at the university seemed trivial and boring to him.

"Sure, and it'd be remarkable for you to develop something for them, but you've been at it for years and haven't made any breakthroughs. No one has. It's impossible."

"It can't be impossible."

"It can and you know it."

"It might be impossible," Ferrun conceded. "But we haven't proved it's impossible; we could make a breakthrough tomorrow."

"You did the right thing," Jeremy said with a sigh. "You know it was the right thing because we were eating here last week when you settled on not renewing it."

"Someone's going to solve it eventually."

"Maybe that someone will be you." Jeremy paused. "*After* you've published some more papers and have tenure and can pursue whatever you want without getting fired for a lack of results."

"Someone will figure it out within the next five years."

"That's what they were saying during our undergrad."

"Dr. Long would have told me to quit if it wasn't realistic," Ferrun said. "That's what bosses are supposed to do, lead you in the right direction."

"Dr. Long has been encouraging you to quit for the past year."

"He's been nothing but supportive."

"Reading your observations on unsuccessful tests isn't support."

Ferrun could only groan in agreement. He wasn't interested in any of the prospective projects. He wanted to make the company's material, not just so his name would be on the patent but because it could really change how things were built for the better. The material could lead to long-term sustainability in that sector.

Every other project just felt bleak and pointless. He didn't care about the hardness of rubber. Some poor undergrad could poke things with a durometer. Unfortunately, he knew doing nothing wasn't going to help his career either.

"Come on, let's play some pool and get our minds off this," Jeremy proposed.

Jeremy got the pool balls from the bartender wearing an eyepatch while Ferrun grabbed his mostly full and mostly warm beer and walked over to the pool table. Jeremy racked the balls and let Ferrun break. The cue ball rolled down the table, and with a crack, the triangular arrangement dissipated and so did the dream.

Chapter Eight

A rguing on the beach, Gesa asked, "Why do you want to focus on building a house first?" After a fresh night's sleep, the pair had no lack of energy, but they disputed what to work on first.

"Just a shelter," Ferrun clarified. "Like a simple lean-to. It would help you, since you're stuck out here in the sun. And it will help us practice building things. We can see how durable our knots are before we start building a hull."

"The sun's not going to bother me. I was lying in the sun while floating across the ocean. I'm not worried about a sunburn."

"But if we build a shelter, we can take breaks," Ferrun continued, "then we won't be as tired. We'll be able to build more and will get this done sooner."

"Sooner," she said with a chuckle. "You think we'll really get this done faster by working on something else? Plus, you are aware we have an eternity to get this done, right? There's no rush."

Ferrun admitted she was right; there was no rush. They could spend years just researching and developing how to tie a knot most efficiently. He just wanted to get on with figuring things out as fast as possible.

"I'll help you build the shelter," she said, looking over at the trees. "It's your rope after all, and I'll admit it would be nice to sit somewhere that isn't in the sun."

"Great!" Ferrun was glad she answered before he had to wrestle with why everything was urgent to him. "Now we just have to figure out how to cut down trees with only ropes and rocks."

***

They made substantial progress on the boat over the past few weeks. Today they were tying logs to the deck of the boat so they could keep their balls of rope corralled as they sailed.

"You know, I'm pretty sure most people would just leave the rope lying on the deck as they travel," Gesa pointed out. She was always teasing Ferrun about the meticulous way he took care of his rope.

"Why? So we can trip, fall overboard, and drown?" Explaining to her the importance of keeping the balls of rope tidy had become a habit since she first started working with his rope. She mocked the religiousness of his practice, but he stood by it, usually saying something like, "When you have all your slack in one place, you'll understand why it's important." They both were silently doubtful that the day would ever come when they would see their rocks.

Ferrun spent the morning cutting down trees with a rudimentary rock ax Gesa had built, using the rope closest to his ankle to drag the wood to the shore. This all happened while Gesa wrapped the previous day's logs with the far end of his rope to make the sides of the boat.

In the heat of the early afternoon, they took a nap in the large lean-to. Then, in the late afternoon and evening, the pair assembled the parts of the boat Gesa had prepared. This was the main two-person task on which they had to work together.

Gesa was in the middle of what Ferrun was confident would be a funny jest when they turned their heads at a splashing sound in the distance. It wasn't the rhythmic patting of the waves on the shore either. They looked up from their work and saw a white figure floating in from the sea.

"Did that person just swim across the ocean?" Gesa asked with more wonder than Ferrun expected from someone who'd achieved it herself.

"I suspect so," Ferrun replied.

"I didn't think anyone else would be dumb enough to do it. You should go talk to them."

Ferrun didn't need much encouragement, and he immediately began climbing off the makeshift deck of the boat. He let out his slack and approached the man on the beach. The man's clothes were soaked, and Ferrun could see through the white linens he wore.

The two men talked for a while. Ferrun explained Gesa's situation and why he was building a boat. The man shared his logic for crossing the ocean, which mirrored Gesa's reasoning. Once the man had caught his breath and his clothes were dry from the sun, he picked up his rope and bid Ferrun farewell. Ferrun watched the man lumber off into the thin woods and towards the mountain. His rope wasn't stuck on the ocean floor like Gesa's was.

When Ferrun returned to the deck of the boat, he filled Gesa in on the conversation as they worked on the knots for the deck.

"And then he just walked away?" she asked.

"Yeah, he wanted to get to the mountain, and he had caught his breath. He was less than interested in going back out on the ocean."

"But he was able to just walk away from the shore like that?" Gesa seemed offended by the unfairness.

"He'll probably get stuck eventually."

"He couldn't have landed thirty ells from where I did, yet he didn't get caught on anything!" Gesa stopped tying the knot in front of her.

Ferrun muttered something about currents and rock sizes, but he knew it wasn't helping.

"It's just not fair. I did everything he did, and he just got to walk away while I'm stuck here building a boat so I can remove my rock from some Aegir's damned depths." Gesa's face was bright red. Her mood was a grand departure from her typical sunny disposition.

"It's not anything you did wrong." He knew this wasn't something she was going to be laughing off any time soon. "These things can't be controlled. I'm sure that once you dislodge your rock, you'll be able to pass him on your way up the mountain." Ferrun had told himself the same thing every time someone laughed at his idea of picking up all his slack.

"I doubt it. If it's not one thing, it will be another. I'll probably get lost on my way to the mountain and spend eternity traveling parallel to its base. Then Loki will just be laughing at this trick he's played on me." She climbed off the boat to stand on the sand.

Ferrun watched her climb down, unsure of what he could say to get her out of this mood. She picked up her rope from the shore and tugged at it.

"Do you want help?" Ferrun asked.

When she growled and cursed at the rope but didn't respond, Ferrun picked up the work where she had left off.

***

Gesa took breaks to tug at her rope for a few days but was soon back to working on the boat full-time. When Ferrun left to gather trees, he would place sticks on the man's rope, and if they had moved the next day, he would know the man was still making progress. He kept the ritual a secret from Gesa, but he was fascinated with the man's journey, and as petty as it was, he hoped to one day report to her that the man had gotten stuck.

After months of building the boat and tracking the progress of the man's rope, Ferrun noticed it had stopped moving. When the stick hadn't moved a few days in a row, he informed Gesa. However, she was unphased by the news.

"Why are you glad that he's stuck?" she asked.

"Because it means I was right. There's some sort of balance to the world, and we're not the only ones stuck."

"Him being stuck is just further proof that this whole world exists to hold us back."

Ferrun continued tying together the logs he was working on. Gesa had made a good point, but he didn't have the luxury of blaming it on the gods. He'd put himself in this position.

Chapter Nine

After what felt like the better part of a year, they finished the boat.

"You know, it's a hell of a step up from what I used to get over here," Gesa said as they looked at it the night before its maiden voyage.

"Thanks for the help," Ferrun said.

"You know, I really thought it was going to be a glorified raft," Gesa said, poking fun at him and his original plans.

Ferrun had worked through everything and probably overengineered plenty of things on it. There was a rudder and a mast, although they had no sail to put on it. His original idea of a lean-to on the boat evolved into an entire cabin between the deck of the ship and the hull. There were some corrals for his rope, and Gesa's as well whenever she started accumulating it.

However, the pride of the whole boat was that he had figured out how to use sap from the trees to waterproof the hull. He didn't have many balls of rope left since they had to use so much of it to tie the logs together, but he knew they'd be accumulating more as they traveled.

As the sun rose the next morning, they loaded up Ferrun's two remaining balls of rope into the corrals to set off to sea.

"I, uh, got something for you," Ferrun said as they pushed the boat into the water. Gesa turned to look at him, her feet firmly planted, eager to push off. "It's a flower I found while collecting wood in the forest." He handed her a purple flower shaped like a champagne glass with the tips of the petals curling back.

"What a unique color it is," Gesa remarked as she looked at it.

"I know you wanted to go into those woods, and I felt bad bringing only wood to you, so I figured I'd grab this before we set off."

"I didn't see anything like it on the other side of the ocean. I wish I had the slack to explore this forest."

"Hopefully one day you will." Ferrun wondered if he would ever come back to this side of the ocean.

Gesa weaved the flower into a braid of her hair. "It'll be safe here." She gave it a light pat and stepped towards him.

Ferrun gave her a hug. He wished he'd done more, but the moment had passed. "Come on, let's push this into the water and get going." He knew how eager she was to free her rock.

***

It took them a while to get out past the waves that pushed them towards the shore, but they pulled on their ropes with all their strength and eventually cleared the current.

Ferrun tied his rope to the deck and took a break. Gesa began wrapping up her slack. She had accumulated a few hundred yards in the process of leaving the shore.

"I really didn't think I would ever see this much of my rope in one place," she said cheerily.

"If you spent a year swimming across the ocean, you're going to wind up seeing a bit more than that." He showed her how to tie it up into a ball. After a bit of fussing, it was in a neat sphere twice the size of her head.

"Well, now it's not nearly as impressive," she complained.

"Don't worry; it will grow," Ferrun said absentmindedly as he untied his rope so they could begin pulling themselves across the ocean again.

A little before sunset, the two sailors ran into a problem. Gesa's rope had split paths from his. Ferrun had feared it would happen as they built the boat but never brought it up. He knew it was out of his control one way or the other.

"What should we do?" he asked her as they tied the ropes to the deck to take a break. If they had two boats, they would have split paths like he did with Teekola. But they were sharing the same boat, and there was no way they could follow both lines.

"I hate to be selfish, but I think we're going to have to follow my line," Gesa responded, eying Ferrun's slack. "You have a bit more slack, and I think we could make good progress towards my rock before you run out."

"What if I run out?" Ferrun tried to imagine the situation where neither of them had the slack to chase a rock.

"We would have to let my line out and get yours. It would be a constant back and forth of tracing one line back, then the other. Eventually, we would get to my rock or the shore."

"We could be out here forever." Between this realization and the thought of the work it would take, Ferrun sank onto the deck to rest.

"It's a good thing we didn't have to pack food," Gesa said with a chuckle. "We've got all eternity. You really should work to grasp that concept," she teased.

***

The next morning, they began letting out Ferrun's slack to find Gesa's rock. They were forced to find a way to automate how Ferrun's line let out slack because Gesa's rope pulled them against the ocean's current. It took both of them to drag the weight of the boat against the tide, and without two people pulling, they would make no progress or lose progress with a misstep.

After they got into the habit of pulling in the rope, the boat made smooth progress across the sea. Ferrun realized that his two balls of rope would give them more distance than he suspected initially because pulling Gesa's line in didn't always require his slack to let the same length out.

Weeks passed as the pair traveled together, and soon idle remarks were not enough to fill a day's worth of conversation. Their being together made the memories of their respective lives come back, and Ferrun found himself recounting fascinating tales of the future to Gesa.

"So you grew up not knowing how to navigate by stars?" Gesa asked, baffled. "You depended on GPX?"

"GPS," Ferrun corrected. "Satellites."

The pair lay on the deck under the clear night sky. Their rope mats were close enough that they could point out constellations they found, although Gesa did most of the finding.

"Yes, yes, the stars you put in the sky."

"Well, I didn't put them there," Ferrun corrected. "I just used them."

"Good thing we don't have to navigate here. Without your stars you'd be lost."

"What did you do?" Ferrun asked. Gesa rarely talked about her past, but her fitful dreams told him she'd remembered some of it, for better or worse.

"I was a storyteller."

"Like an author?"

"A priestess," Gesa corrected. "I studied the stars, and the wind, and the birds that flew in from the sea."

"To tell stories."

"To tell my tribe what the goddess wanted from them." Her tone was melancholy. "But it wasn't always true."

"How could it be? We're in the afterlife and have spoken to only one god. They're aloof at best."

"I heard my goddess clearly. Through the leaves in the wind, and the way the flames danced when consuming sacrifices. But I heard the chief clearly as well."

"What did he have to say?"

"That there were Welsh and Anglo-Saxons to fight, and other tribes to challenge."

"And your goddess?" Ferrun asked, unsure of how to phrase the question.

"She would have preferred to leave them alone."

"I'm sure she had her reasons."

Gesa made a humph sound at this. "I'm sure she did. But I told the tribe what they wanted to hear. Said the goddess blessed their travels and their wars."

"And that didn't go well?" Ferrun could hardly remember the barbaric wars he'd learned about in history classes.

"It went great," Gesa said with a light laugh. "I didn't even feel bad."

"Well, maybe you just misunderstood your goddess."

"Two moons later war came to our village. They'd heard we had hoards from our campaigns and came with overwhelming numbers." Gesa shook her head as if to make the memory go away.

"You don't have to talk about it if you don't want."

"What else is there to say? I died in the fight. Sometimes I'm burned in the temple, sometimes I'm stabbed fighting back, sometimes it's worse."

"I'm sorry," Ferrun said.

"In some dreams, I am faithful to the goddess. Unfortunately, other priestesses override me. Or the chief ignores my pleas. Someone comes in the end. And I'm left wondering how I wound up here. In an afterlife unlike anything I'd imagined."

"I wish I had an answer for that."

"But what are you going to do?" Her tone draped happiness over her previously somber tone. "I'm back out on the sea, this time on a boat. And the company isn't half bad."

"Thanks," Ferrun said with a grin. "I think Yore-mond-gang is rising over there." He pointed at the stars in a constellation she'd named.

"It's Jörmungandr." She pronounced the last syllable with a *ch* sound, which Ferrun had yet to master.

***

One early morning before the sun was up, Ferrun woke with the realization that his boulder might be at the bottom of the ocean as well. And if his rock was the biggest one the gods had on this world, then there would be no way to move it.

After sharing this fearful realization with Gesa, she responded with, "Well, if it's as big as you say it is, then that will mean you'll probably get your own private island. You and your balls of rope can just hang out there and wait for castaways like me to float by. Maybe I'll even come to visit you after I make it up the mountain and they make me a Valkyrie."

However, as dawn came on them that day, they realized they had a much bigger problem to face. On the horizon were slate-gray storm clouds streaked with black shadows. The blue sky they were floating under was cut off by the dark clouds. They could see lightning going off inside them, but they were still too far away to hear any thunder.

"I didn't know this world had such weather," Ferrun said.

Gesa sighed. "This would be my luck. I finally start making some progress towards being unstuck, and Thor throws a party." She sat down, leaning against the side of the boat.

Ferrun inspected their crudely made boat and had some doubts of its ability to survive a drizzle, let alone a massive lightning storm like the one on the horizon.

"Could we go around it?" Ferrun eyed the rudder they built but hadn't used.

"I don't think so," she answered in a small voice as the wind picked up, "and even if we could, I'm sure we would just run into some other issue."

Ferrun realized there was one thing they still had that could help them survive this situation. He began pulling in as much slack from his rope as possible. When it was taut, he tied it to the opposite side of the boat as Gesa's line. He then double-checked her rope, making sure the line was taut and they had tightly fastened it to the wood of the boat.

The storm was moving towards them fast, and the wind had picked up so much that his white linen shirt was billowing like a sail. Ferrun looked at Gesa, who hadn't moved since realizing the storm's power.

"Gesa, let's get under the deck." Ferrun grabbed her arm to help her up.

"Why? It's not like the storm will kill us. It might shock us a little and make us wet." Her face looked pitiful.

"Because..." Ferrun started but failed to find a good reason to get under the deck. "Because if we're under the deck, we won't fall overboard and won't have to swim back to the boat after this is over."

Gesa got up but didn't say anything. Perhaps she was too tired to think of a retort to his poor excuse.

They climbed down the small ladder that took them out of the wind. Ferrun looked at the hole in the deck they had entered through and realized that, despite his meticulous planning, he had forgotten something in the design of their boat.

"I don't have a way to close that," he said to Gesa, but she wasn't listening.

Then the rain started to fall, soft for a few seconds, but soon it came down in buckets. Ferrun looked down at his wet feet, realizing that the waterproofing of his hull was about to be their downfall.

Chapter Ten

Cold water rose to Ferrun's ankles. No longer slumping in the corner, Gesa stood next to him with her pants already soaked.

"You have any ideas yet?" Gesa asked.

"We need to plug that hole."

A flash of lightning lit up the cabin. The sound of thunder immediately followed. The rain fell harder, and water from the deck started pouring in through the open hatch.

"Do you think the rope would cover it?" She had to shout over the patter of rain on the deck. "It might soak through, but—"

A flash of lightning followed by deafening thunder cut her off. The rain was unceasing, and the water level was climbing up their legs fast.

Ferrun looked up and noticed there was water leaking between the logs of the deck as well. "Even if we plug that hole, it will still seep in. This boat is going to sink in no time."

The boat rocked from side to side as the wind outside picked up. Ferrun had to put his hand on the wall of the cabin to keep from falling face-first into the pool of water at his feet. As the boat rocked, the tugging on his ankle told him the balls of rope weren't stationary.

"It's only a matter of time before this thing capsizes and we're thrown overboard," Gesa said. "Unless the boat fills up and sinks first."

Ferrun couldn't stop any of that, but he could stop them from getting separated from the boat. He scrambled up the ladder and tied Gesa's rope to the mast a few yards away from her ankle. It was long enough that she'd have some slack, and it would keep her on board even if her rope wasn't. Then he did the same thing for himself.

The wind pushed him around the deck when he wasn't holding onto something, and everything he grabbed was slick from the heavy rain. Ferrun scanned the horizon, but there was no blue sky in sight. They were in the middle of a storm that reached to the horizon.

He climbed back down the ladder, hearing a splash when his foot reached the last rung. The boat kept rocking back and forth. It was almost enough to make him sick.

Gesa was throwing herself against the walls of the hull with each swelling wave. The boat leaned far to one side but then quickly balanced itself. It gave Ferrun a sense of vertigo.

"What the hell are you doing?"

"We need to flip it," Gesa stated matter-of-factly.

"We what?" he asked over the clatter of the rain.

"We need to flip it so it will quit filling up with water. And we need to do it before it gets too heavy."

"But we'll lose our rope that's on deck," he protested, "and we might never get it upright again."

"Definitely," Gesa agreed. "But if it fills with water, we'll never raise it from the bottom of the ocean. And all your rope is weaved into the walls. You'd be stuck here floating aimlessly for eternity. We need to keep this boat above water."

The two sailors felt the swell of another wave pull them. Ferrun joined her at the wall, and they pushed, attempting to flip the boat.

After three attempts, the water reached past their knees and the boat was still upright. They began to jump and throw themselves against the wall with the fourth wave, and the boat began to lose its balance.

Ferrun felt like dice being thrown across a table. The pair rolled around in darkness, eventually landing on what used to be the ceiling. The boat had none of the balance it once had. They now rocked more than they had when it was right side up. On the bright side, the water was no longer climbing up their legs. They were still knee-deep in water, but it wasn't rising.

They rocked back and forth for hours. In the pitch-black, there was no way to keep track of time. They couldn't lie down to sleep and so had to pass the time talking about how to get the boat upright again once the storm was over. Occasionally, they had to pause to let the thunder speak its piece.

"You know," Gesa said as they stood together in the dark, "your ability to get into terrible situations is starting to rub off on me. Who'd ever think I'd try to solve a problem by creating a new one. Just like you and that giant boulder of yours."

Ferrun thought about what she said as they listened to the rain pour onto the hull. "I wonder who I learned it from."

"It's gotten you this far, for better or worse. Hopefully, it will get you up the mountain."

"Or at least to my boulder," Ferrun said, leaning against the hull and staring into the pitch-black of the cabin.

***

Gesa woke Ferrun up from a fitful dream about a fight with his sister. He startled awake, blinking his eyes, trying to get a world to appear in front of him. He was still leaning against the hull. The water was up to his waist. His sleepiness soon faded enough for him to remember where he was.

"What's up?" he asked.

"We're not rocking anymore."

Ferrun's inner ear agreed with Gesa's observation. There was still the gentle back and forth motion that he'd gotten used to in the past month of ocean travel, but they were no longer in the middle of a storm.

"Let's get this thing right side up again," Gesa said.

"Let's get out first." He crawled along the hull until he was able to find the hatch that used to lead to the deck but now opened into the ocean. "It's over here," he called out in the darkness. Gesa made her way to him. They took a deep breath and slid under their capsized boat.

Ferrun opened his eyes underwater and immediately regretted it. The salt stung, but it was the only way he could see where he needed to go. Light shone all around the boat, and he was quickly able to lead himself out from under the hull. When he broke the surface of the water, he sucked in a deep breath of fresh air. Gesa broke the water right behind him.

Their eyes adjusted to the light, and they looked at the upside-down boat. Their hull was less than smooth, which allowed them climb up the sides. With a little effort, they were able to climb to the new top of their boat.

The only damage the boat sustained was the unused rudder. The clump of wood was drifting nearby, tethered to the boat by some loose rope that had untangled from its logs.

"I'd say she did pretty well," Ferrun said, admiring their craftsmanship. "Aside from being upside down."

"You know where all our rope is, right?" Gesa asked as she sat down on the hull.

Ferrun nodded. "It was moving around too much and was going overboard anyway. It wasn't tied down."

Gesa tugged at the rope attached to her ankle. "It was tied to something."

Ferrun joined her cross-legged on the hull. He let out a large sigh and looked at the clear sky. "At least there won't be another storm anytime soon."

"No, I'm sure they'll wait until we get situated and start making progress again before making another one."

"Maybe," Ferrun admitted, "but we're not going to sit here for eternity. We'd drive each other mad. All we have to do is roll the boat and retrieve our rope. Then we'll be on our way to getting your rock and heading up the mountain."

"You really think that's going to happen?" Gesa asked in disbelief.

"It will be tricky, but with some clever rope work, we could get her upright." Ferrun was already inspecting the sides of the boat for a tie-off point.

"No, I mean make it to the top of the mountain."

"Oh..." Ferrun realized they were having two different conversations. "I don't know if I can do it. But I had a friend who told me the key is to prioritize problems and solve them as they come up."

"Good, so it *is* just willful ignorance." Gesa lay down on her back. The sun dried their clothes. "No matter what I do, I wind up in another tough spot. Cross the ocean because it's my only option, and I get stuck. Face a thunderstorm at sea, and we wind up with a capsized boat. Gods only know what I'll face if we get to my rock."

"What else are you supposed to do?"

"I don't know," Gesa said. "And I'm not even in the worst of it. You've got an immovable boulder. I have no idea how you face every day in this eternity."

"At least I signed up for these problems," Ferrun said. "You keep getting dragged into stuff. But what are you going to do?"

"Life was hard, and now apparently the afterlife is hard too. Why'd the gods create us just to be tortured?" Gesa sighed. "Wouldn't we be better off just staying still and not trying anything risky?"

"I can't stay still for eternity. I probably can't even stay still for this afternoon." Ferrun's comment got a short-lived smile out of Gesa. "So I move in the only direction that I can, towards my boulder. And, sure, it's taken me away from the goal, but I've gained a sort of freedom in the process. I have slack! I can move without dragging something behind me."

"The gods keep putting stumbling blocks in my way and yours. You're just unable to see them as aggressions towards you."

"I spent my life not believing these gods existed. So, yeah, it's a little hard to take what happens personally."

"That storm wasn't natural; it was someone powerful bullying us. And that's not fair."

"No, it's not," Ferrun admitted. "But maybe things will change if you make it to the top of the mountain."

"Maybe," Gesa said. "If they let me get there. And maybe it will just lead to the gods assigning me more challenges."

"Possibly." Ferrun had a hard time imagining what life would be like without some problem in front of him to solve.

***

It took them longer than the afternoon to get the boat upright. The pair fell over the side of the hull a few times, but their rope tied to the mast let them find their way back to the boat. After a few days of experimenting with their copious slack and using some tricky rope work, they eventually pulled the boat upright in the water.

The next challenge was to get their rope back on board. The knots Ferrun had tied before the storm continued to hold the boat in place. They spent an entire morning reeling in their rope. By early afternoon, Gesa had gathered up all of her rope and was knotting it into an organized ball. Ferrun, on the other hand, was having trouble. They combined their forces, but even after tugging at it all evening, it refused to come loose.

"I'm going to have to dive down and unknot it from whatever it's stuck on, aren't I?" Ferrun said as they lay on the deck, staring up at the starry night sky.

It took Gesa some time to reply, and when she did, all she said was, "They're bullies. You just don't see it."

"How deep do you think it is?" Ferrun asked, ignoring her comment.

"We're in the middle of the ocean. It's probably bottomless."

"If it's bottomless, then what's my rope and your rock stuck on?" Ferrun tried to reconcile her claim with reality.

"Bad luck," was Gesa's only response. After that, neither had much to add to the evening's conversation.

Chapter Eleven

Ferrun spent the early morning pointlessly pulling on his rope in a last-ditch attempt to avoid having to swim to the bottom of the ocean. But he gave up before the sun had finished rising and accepted the inevitable.

"Just make sure that my rope isn't taut as I swim down," Ferrun instructed. "The last thing I want to do is be an arm's length away from the knot and not have the slack to get it. Especially when I have that massive thing." He gestured at the damp ball of rope they had pulled up the day before.

"I can do that," Gesa said. "The part I have an issue with is pulling you back up after the fact. How will I know when to reel you in?"

"I've been thinking about that too. I don't think you should."

"You don't think I should pull you up?"

"Exactly."

Gesa looked like he'd just asked her to eat tree bark.

"I figure I will make it to the bottom, untie the knot, but after that the chances are low that I'll be able to make it back to the surface in one breath. On the bright side...dead bodies float. All you'll have to do is drag me onto the deck and wait for me to resurrect."

"Are you sure that's what will happen?" Gesa face revealed her disgust. "Have you died before?"

"At least once. That's what got me here."

"No, in this world."

"I met a man who'd hung himself from a tree. He came back to life after we removed the noose that had strangled him. If you can get the water out of my lungs, this world will take care of the rest."

"And if I can't?"

"He also woke up every morning anyway. Just like how our wounds heal with the sunrise. Although I might have a lot of coughing to do when I wake up." Ferrun's mouth cut into a thin smile at his attempt to make light of his potential death.

"I don't like this," Gesa said.

"Me neither, but I don't have a better answer."

"It could take hours for your body to float to the surface, or you could get stuck on something like your rope has, or the tide might take you somewhere far away. I don't want to sit idly by while I wait for your body to come to the surface."

Ferrun frowned with the corners of his mouth. "Yeah, me neither."

"I'll tug on your rope every few seconds. If you tug back, that means you're still swimming down and alive. If you don't kick back, then I will pull you in. I can resurrect you if I have to, but hopefully you'll still be alive and we can try again if we have to."

"I really hope I don't have to die more than once."

"I'm hoping you don't die in the first place."

Gesa's typical cheery attitude she had on the beach had faded with their time at sea, and Ferrun saw she was as scared as he was. Then he realized it was because what happened to him could happen to her when she went to dive for her rock—assuming they ever got Ferrun's rope unstuck in the first place.

***

Ferrun gasped for breath. The air was salty and cold as it filled his lungs. Then he began to cough again. He felt like he was heaving buckets of salt water out of his lungs even though only a few puddles had landed on the deck of their makeshift boat. After a few more cycles of breathing and coughing, Ferrun finally had recovered enough to take in his surroundings.

Gesa was sitting on the other side of the boat with her arms wrapped around her knees. She stared at Ferrun with haunted eyes. If that look was from seeing him die and come back to life, then his own face must have looked twice as bad.

He tried to put on a smile as he looked across the deck at her, but it quickly faded. After drowning and recovering the first time, she asked him what it was like.

"You know those dreams we have here about our past that cement themselves as memories?"

She nodded.

"It's like those but worse." He didn't know how the hanged man found comfort in them.

Gesa shuddered. She avoided talking about her past, and he didn't want to dig into bitter memories.

"The dreams always turn to nightmares. I'm either paralyzed or helpless. If I try to uncover something about my past, I'm distracted or it's obscured. Then when the dream is over, I'm left in this darkness—complete and utter darkness."

"That's no worse than being in the boat when it was upside down," she said, trying to make the most of the situation.

"It's much worse. My mind feels like it is being stretched to infinity. It wouldn't be all that bad if I weren't also burdened by a sense of...I don't know...self. In this void, I don't think I'm supposed to be me; I'm supposed to be"—Ferrun gestured out to sea—"everything."

He wondered if the dark void he had passed into was where his consciousness was supposed to be recycled for other beings as Merc had explained when he first arrived in this world. Unfortunately, when Ferrun died in this world and crossed into the black, his mind was kept together, and he was unequipped to face the void's expanse.

Gesa was polite enough not to push the subject further, and she lowered him down for another trip when he was ready.

***

"How are you feeling?" Gesa asked in a tone that was as subtle as the waves patting the side of the boat.

Ferrun didn't have the energy to lie. They had tried to reach the knot at the bottom of the ocean three times that day, and each time it had ended with him coming back to life on the deck.

"I feel like clay flattened then compressed into a ball. In case it wasn't apparent, drowning isn't enjoyable." He cracked a small smile, but reality quickly fought it off. "It's like experiencing everything and nothing at the same time. My mind can't do it." He paused at his phrasing. "Not that I have a mind, brain, or body when I die. I simply have the sense that I'm one speck in the infinite darkness." He shuddered as an evening breeze blew across the deck and cooled his soaking wet clothes.

"Curse the gods for doing this to us," Gesa said with a fury in her eyes. "They're bastards for torturing you like this. It's what we get for attempting their challenge in an even remotely intelligent way."

"It's our fault, not theirs," Ferrun said calmly. "We didn't prepare for every eventuality. We should have kept our rope underdeck, where it wouldn't fall off." He looked at the sun's position in the sky.

"I don't think we have time to try again before dark," Gesa said, knowing how dedicated he was to solving the problem as soon as possible. "And even if we did…" She trailed off in thought.

Ferrun finished her sentence. "I don't know how much good it would do. I haven't made it deep enough to see what my rope is stuck on."

"You know, we have a saying: Tyr only offered up his hand once."

"What's that mean?"

"You'd be crazy to do the same thing twice and expect a different outcome."

"If I'm crazy, it's because of that void. I don't know how the hanged man does it."

"And he woke up every morning only to face it again," Gesa said, remembering Ferrun's story. "Like getting a gasp of breath only to be drowned again."

"That's not a bad idea."

"Excuse me?" Gesa blinked at him in surprise.

"I'm never going to make it to the bottom of the ocean in one breath. We've proved it's impossible. But if I died, sank to the bottom, and resurrected in the morning, I'd have the morning breath to fix it."

Gesa stared at him in horror as if she were facing down another storm. "You want to die to fix this? Why would you drag yourself through more torture?"

"It's going to suck, sure, but we've got to get unstuck. And this is the best idea we've got."

Gesa stared at him, probably formulating an argument against his wild plan.

Ferrun spoke before she could come up with anything. "Shockingly I'm not a big fan of dying either. That void is a nightmare. But I'm even less eager to sit here for eternity. Drowning is an option, and we owe it to ourselves to explore all possible options before we give up."

"As much as I want to blame the gods, sometimes I feel you put yourself in these torturous situations," Gesa said with a frown.

***

The sun was setting as they finished wrapping the rope around Ferrun. He was covered in the sinking rope, and they hoped it would hold him to the ocean floor so he could unknot his rope from whatever was down there.

"You look like a ball of rope grew arms and legs," Gesa said with a small laugh.

Ferrun smiled and tried to look down at himself, but the thick layers of rope kept his head from moving much. "I hope this works." He waddled to the side of the boat. The waves shone orange in the dim light of the setting sun.

"Me too. It's going to be lonely up here without you."

"It's going to be lonely down there too." Ferrun was actively ignoring the fact that he would have to face the void alone as well—this time for longer than before, if that was how time worked on the other side.

The two travelers double-checked the knots that would keep him on course as he sank. Then Gesa checked that his wrapping was tight enough that he would sink but loose enough that she could pull it up when he was done.

Ferrun stood at the edge of the boat. The sun was gone, and the dim light of dusk was fading. He was as ready as he'd ever be. He looked at Gesa one last time, and he met her eyes.

"Good luck," she said with a smile, then gave him a short kiss.

"Thanks," he said as a grin grew across his face. He took a deep breath of the cool evening air and leaned back, falling off the side of the boat.

He sank far faster than he ever could have swum. He even thought he might be able to make it to the bottom before he ran out of oxygen. However, as he sank deeper and the ocean got darker, the rope that ran towards the ocean floor showed no sign of stopping. Ferrun began to lose hope of reaching it on his first breath.

His lungs burned for air. Every molecule of oxygen in his chest was used up, and he needed more. His body urged him to inhale, but he fought it. He grew tired and confused, sinking into the pitch-black depths of the ocean. The pressure of the water around him was weighing on his eardrums, and he wondered if Gesa were right about the ocean being bottomless. Ferrun gasped for breath, desperate and unable to hold himself back. His lungs filled with salty water. He coughed, but it only released air, making more room for the suffocating water. The darkness encompassed him.

Chapter Twelve

He faced the black void, bodiless and incoherent. He was being pulled to fill the dark vacuum of infinity around him, but he couldn't do it. His ego was stretched in every direction for eternity.

After what felt like moments and eternity at the same time, he faced darkness with an unbearable weight on his chest. His chest was desperate for air, and he took a small breath. Ages of bodily reflexes moved faster than his mind. Ferrun inhaled salty water and coughed it back out. Air bubbles followed, but he could only feel them slip by his face. His lungs burned for fresh air, but tons of water separated him from it.

His hands went to the rope that tethered the boat to the ocean floor. He felt his rope stuck on a rough object, likely a rock. *My rock?* he wondered. He tugged at it, but it was tight and slippery.

Ferrun felt his head go light. He was going to lose consciousness again. Frantically, he fiddled with the rope before his body forced him to inhale a deep breath of salt water. He wedged his fingers between the rope and the rock to anchor himself.

***

Ferrun finished his second drink, both of them free so far. Jeremy brought him another one while Ferrun talked with Dr. Long. An older grad student, whom Jeremy was advising, had joined them, wearing a ridiculous Hawaiian shirt, but Ferrun couldn't remember his name. The four of them were playing pool.

"It took you three years, but you finally figured it out." Jeremy congratulated him for the umpteenth time that night.

Dr. Long struck the cue ball, but the angle was too wide, and the striped yellow ball missed the pocket. It was now Ferrun's turn.

"What helped you crack it and figure it out?" the grad student asked after Ferrun had finished his shot. Only Dr. Long and Jeremy had read the paper so far, but it'd be published soon.

"Well, all I had to do was…" Ferrun paused. He tried to remember how he found the formula for the construction company's material. The only thing that came to mind was emptiness, an uncomfortable darkness he didn't want to face. It must have been the beer. "You can read the paper. It goes into more detail than I could right now." He gave the guy a smile as Jeremy took his shot, sinking a ball.

"Who let you two be on a team together?" Ferrun complained, trying to take his mind off the uncomfortable subject of his success.

"I haven't gotten any balls in so far," Dr. Long admitted.

"Only because you're going easy on me. Not that I don't appreciate it."

"Can you believe you weren't going to submit the renewal a few years back?" Jeremy said. "I think we were eating over there." He gestured at an empty table with his pool cue. "I said, 'Ferruccio Mortimer Monteiro, you submit that paperwork tonight before you go to sleep.'"

"You did not," Ferrun scoffed. "My middle name is Vincent, and you said I should save my job and pursue something else."

"They can't fire you now," Jeremy said, raising his mug.

"We could probably find a way," Dr. Long said. "But it'd make the university look bad. The funding that patent is going to bring..." He shook his head in wonder at what it could do.

"I just can't believe you figured it out," the grad student said. "We thought it'd be another ten years until anyone made significant progress on it. What kept you going on the project even though it seemed hopeless?"

"It was the money," Jeremy replied with a laugh.

"No," Ferrun said, although he knew that wouldn't hurt. "It was just a project I agreed to start, and I wanted to see it to the end." He took a sip of his beer. "Whose turn is it?"

"Yours," Jeremy said, pointing his cue at him.

Ferrun took a shot and sunk a ball into a corner pocket.

"What was different when you finally got the results you were af-ter?" Jeremy asked.

"It had to have been luck." Ferrun hated the words as they came out of his mouth. "I just kept trying different things, and one day things started to go my way."

"What made you try the final formula?" the grad student asked.

Ferrun tried to keep a happy face on, but the guy wouldn't let up. He couldn't blame him; he'd do the same in this situation.

"Sleep deprivation," Dr. Long said. "Some of the best break-throughs I've ever seen were from sleep deprivation."

"Have you planned a Nobel Prize speech yet?" Jeremy asked.

"Oh, come on. You're acting like I cured cancer. I just figured out how to..." Ferrun wasn't sure how to finish the sentence.

"Make the most remarkable construction material since concrete," Jeremy said before Ferrun could find the words.

Ferrun looked at the chaotic array of balls on the table, then to the people around the table. The face across from him, the grad student's, was strange to him; he'd never met the guy before, at least not at the school. Jeremy's hair was shorter than he'd ever seen it, and Dr. Long had a gray beard instead of a salt-and-pepper one. These weren't the people he'd always worked with. They were people he knew, but they were aged and nearly unrecognizable.

Ferrun tried to remember what he did that night after Jeremy had told him to pursue something else. He had a memory of not doing anything at all and giving up the project. He remembered discussing his progress with Dr. Long. He remembered dreading going into work because of the lack of progress he'd made. His memory was scattered like the balls on the table.

The black eight ball was now the only thing on the table. A wrinkle-faced Dr. Long gestured to him. "Your shot."

Ferrun didn't know where all the other balls had gone or when it'd become his turn again, but he always had a hard time keeping up with such things, especially after a few drinks. He leaned over the table and stared at the black ball. The eight was on the top and bottom, so it was a nearly complete black sphere.

"What did you have to give up and sacrifice to get to the solution?" the grad student asked. "Surely it was more than just some sleep."

Ferrun wondered what the opportunity had cost him. He tried to think back to the details of the past few years. Not just the details of the lab and the solution, which were fuzzy, but also his family, relationships, hobbies. The only thing there was a memory of a bus stop, and he shook his head, making that memory fade away as well.

He looked at the ball, trying to focus on his shot. It was straightforward. He just had to avoid sinking the cue ball as well. He'd made similar shots a hundred times.

"Anything you wish you had done instead for the past few years?" the grad student asked.

No, there wasn't anything he'd rather be doing. Of course, that was from the hindsight of having solved the problem. What hadn't he done in the past few years? Nothing rang out. It was empty. It was more than empty; it was dark as well.

Then one thing echoed out like a bell in a cavern. There was one thing he wished he'd done. He wished he had helped the little girl in the street. What was her name? It started with an *E*—no, an *A*...

He looked at the ball again, trying to get that horrific morning out of his mind. The ball seemed to grow. The blackness of it rose up to his size. He stood back, trying to hold it off with the pool cue, but it engulfed him. The noise from the bar, the questions from his friends, and the game he was about to win faded as he faced the impenetrable void.

***

The knot's size was hidden in the darkness. The loops were tightly knitted together and hard to trace with his fingers. He fought with the knot and his desire to breathe. The dark depths of the ocean made it impossible to track his progress. After what felt like hours of fighting, he couldn't take it anymore. He inhaled salty water, and his consciousness went into the waiting void.

Memories and dreams washed over him. Nightmares of being torn apart by animals, buses, and the forces of space. He was not made to face any of them. Over time his sense of self eroded. The knot's hold loosened as the mind that was once so confidently Ferrun eroded.

It didn't remember what it was. Memories and ideas tossed about in the darkness. Countless times it failed to undo the rope and was thrown back to places it didn't belong.

Then out of nowhere, the last of the rope slipped free from the rocky depths. Ferrun was rewarded for success by being thrown once again into the dark void.

***

The darkness subsided, and Ferrun heard a man shouting at him. "It's not that easy. It cost me a lot to raise you kids."

The man was Vito, Ferrun's father, and the two were at the grave of Ferrun's mother, Susan, a neutral ground but not short on emotions.

"I know, Padre," Ferrun said. "I know it wasn't easy. But Emilia moved out eight years ago."

"And I'm still paying her bills."

"I'm paying her bills," Ferrun said. It came out harsher than he'd meant it.

"You don't send her money." He wagged his finger to scold Ferrun.

"I send you money. You're an accountant; you should be better at this."

"It's one thing managing money for a big firm; it's another thing managing what little they pay me."

"Then apply elsewhere." Ferrun waved his hands around as if every gravestone in the yard were hiring.

"I can't. This place has been good to me."

"You've been with them my whole life. Apply for a promotion."

His father groaned. It wasn't the first time Ferrun had pitched the idea. "It's not easy like your job. I can't just go back to school and get promoted."

"That wasn't easy for me either. And you can go back to school."

"I know more than the *stronzi* teaching the class." Vito made a rude gesture to no one in particular.

"Then ace it and move up."

"I don't have the money."

"Padre..." Ferrun's frustration made it sound like a curse. "I got through school with scholarships. So did Mateo and Gabriella."

"There's no scholarships for an old man like me." His shoulders slumped as if his arms held hundred-pound weights.

"There are, and they'll help you."

"We're famiglia. We have to help each other."

Ferrun swallowed. He was less prepared than he wanted to be. "I can't keep supporting you."

"Gabriella has the kids, and Mateo is in another state. You're going to abandon me like the rest of them?"

"I'm not abandoning you. I just can't afford to keep helping."

"*Cacare,*" his father cursed, waving his hand as if to make the claim disappear. "You're doing great. You just got the new job at the university."

"And living downtown is expensive."

"Live with me. The house is huge."

"I'm not moving back in with you and driving an hour to work."

"I can't keep up with it myself."

Ferrun threw his hands above his head. "Then sell it!"

"It's in pieces. I can't keep up with it myself."

"I'm done solving your problems. I have enough problems to solve with this new research, and I can't keep taking on yours."

"You're my son. You're going to let me starve and grow old alone?"

Ferrun groaned and didn't try to hide it. "Padre, you're not going to starve. I'll be around on Sundays for dinner, and we'll still talk on the phone, but I'm not lending you any more money."

"Money is what buys the food."

"Then quit spending it on stupid stuff." Ferrun gestured at his dad's new car. He felt bad leaving his father with his problems, but the man had started the habit of avoiding them when Ferrun was a kid. He wasn't confident that cutting his old man off would break the practice. But he'd tried everything else.

***

Ferrun wretched salt water onto the wooden deck. His stomach and lungs heaved to expel the water they'd absorbed. Coughing and gasping passed for breathing as he took in fresh air for the first time in forever. After catching his breath, he fell back onto the deck and stared at the blue expanse above him. Robbed of light for so long, he was glad to be free of the darkness.

Ferrun sat up to look across the deck at Gesa. She looked worried, and damp rope lay everywhere. "Are you okay?" he asked.

She looked at him, bewildered. Then a small smile crawled across her lips. "You're in a hell of a place to ask that. You've been underwater for a moon's turn."

She walked across the deck and sat down next to him. She wrapped her arm around him, and he felt her warmth. The sun was warm, the air was warm, and she was warm.

The depths of the ocean and his mind were cold, lonely, and dark. He huddled closer to her for warmth. She had saved him, and she had helped him. If it weren't for her, he would be stuck. If it weren't for him, she would be stuck.

"Curse the gods for doing this to you," Gesa said as he lay in her arms.

It took Ferrun a moment to make sense of her statement. "The gods didn't do that to me. These gods you keep blaming saved us from that darkness. We aren't prepared to enter. They saved us from becoming nothing."

"By doing what? Holding us back here with ropes and rocks?"

"By letting us be ourselves a little longer, and giving us a chance to be with others, because it seems that the alternative is an infinite loneliness." Revisiting the idea sent chills down his back.

He nuzzled into her warmth, glad to be in the sun with someone else. He didn't want to be alone.

Chapter Thirteen

Ferrun's rope came up easily after his dark descent to the ocean floor. A few of his experiences from the deep stuck in his mind like memories, but most faded like a long dream.

It took them months to pull in the rest of Gesa's rope, but neither of them was in a hurry. They faced a few more storms, but none as bad as the first. The rope stayed under the deck now, where it wouldn't roll off.

Neither of them could understand how they had traveled so far without the other. The sailing brought the couple closer together. Ferrun was actively ignoring the thought of having to be eventually separated from Gesa if he ever wanted to reach their goal of the mountain. He could tell she was doing the same.

When the day came that they ran out of rope for Gesa to pull in, neither of them had expected it. If they had counted the rope balls, they would have known the boat was getting close to its destination. However, they were both too preoccupied with each other to notice.

They tried to heave the rock up from the depths of the ocean, but after hours of effort, it still wouldn't move.

"I'm going to have to go down there," Gesa said with a sigh. She plopped down on the deck.

Like a partially healed wound, Ferrun remembered his fear and pain from the depths. He knew he didn't want to face it again, nor did he want anyone else to have to experience it—least of all, the woman he had come to love.

***

Ferrun leaned over the side of the boat as Gesa treaded water with a rope harness wrapped over her shoulders and under her arms.

"I don't think I can do it," she shouted so he could hear her over the waves.

Ferrun gave her a frown. "Why not? Is it too deep?" He was balancing on their small boat cluttered with the few dozen balls that no longer fit under the deck.

Gesa shook her head. "I'm too slow swimming down, and my armpits are starting to ache. I think if I use the tether rope instead of swimming, that might help. She dove down again, and Ferrun waited. This dive would be her fourth attempt.

When she'd emerged initially, Gesa cursed the gods for burying the rock so deep under the water. Ferrun had attempted to point out that the gods merely attached her leg to the boulder and that the knot he had to untie was much deeper, but she unsurprisingly didn't want to hear it. Now he was merely trying to help her in any way he could.

Gesa and Ferrun were both worried about her drowning. Thinking through the situation, Gesa had realized that she would have to spend half her time swimming back for air unless she could swim up faster than she went down. To help her return to the surface quicker, she created a harness out of some of her rope. With the harness, Ferrun could help pull her up when she was close to out of breath.

In his hands, the line Ferrun held went taut a few times, then began to go slack. Gesa was swimming back up. He pulled the rope in as fast as he could to help her get to the surface fast enough.

Gesa broke the surface and gasped for air. Ferrun tied the rope off as she caught her breath so she didn't have to work as hard to stay above water.

"Any luck?" he called out.

She shook her head, still breathing heavily. She was shivering a bit despite the warm sun beating down on them.

"Do you want to come back up here?" Ferrun offered.

"No, I think I was close. Give me one more shot."

Once she caught her breath, Ferrun gave her some slack, and she dived down again. Ferrun felt it took less time for her to tug for his help this round, and he began pulling her up. Moments later, she climbed the rope ladder to get out of the water and was lying on the deck in her soaked white linens and absorbing as much heat from the sun as she could.

"I think I was really close on the last try."

"How could you tell?" Ferrun wasn't able to add up the timeline in his head. Unless she had learned to swim faster, he couldn't see how she might have gotten closer. "Did you see the rock or something?"

"No, I just kind of felt like I was closer." She gave him a slight shrug. "And it felt like I swam further."

Ferrun shrugged.

"You don't think so?" She sounded offended.

"Neither of us has a watch, so we can't tell for sure." Ferrun tried to avoid an argument. "I just feel you're going to have to do something to get yourself down there faster." He failed to mention the option of doing the same crazy thing he had. He hoped her rock wasn't stuck so tightly that she'd have to do that.

"I don't want to be drowned for a month," she said meekly. "I just want to unjam my rock and come up in one breath. Is that too hard to ask?"

"If we had my rock, or any rock, you could hold it and sink to the bottom to get it."

"Or we could just throw a ball of rope off the deck and sacrifice a few months of progress so I can get to the ocean floor in one breath." She cracked a smile at her own jest.

"You know, that's not the worst idea."

Gesa laughed a deep laugh that contrasted her sour mood. "You think throwing all this rope off the boat would help?"

"At least some of it. It sinks, and you need to go down faster."

"Yeah, it would help, but what happens when it gets knotted at the bottom, or I get stuck under it, or we run out of balls to throw over?"

Ferrun didn't have any answers, and he suspected that this was why he wound up in so many challenging situations.

*　*　*

Gesa stood at the edge of the boat in the morning sun, holding a ball of rope the size of her wingspan.

"I hope this thing doesn't unravel on the way down," Ferrun said. They'd brainstormed some solutions to Gesa's concerns and figured they didn't have anything better to try than sinking her with the rope ball.

"There are about a dozen things I'm hoping won't go wrong on my way down," Gesa said as Ferrun checked that the knot holding the harness to her was tight enough. "But the only way we'll find out if this is going to work is if we do it. As soon as I go over the edge, it's in the hands of the gods."

Ferrun turned her around to face him. The ball of rope came between them, but he held eye contact with her. "Gesa, whatever happens down there, up here, all around"—he gestured to the sea and the horizon—"it's all under your control. You can control either what happens to you or how you react. But don't go down into that water thinking it's not up to you. If you do, then you've already lost. I love you, and I want to see you free. I want to see you next to your boulder."

"Sure, thanks," Gesa said flatly. She turned her back to him, took a deep breath, and stepped off the side of the boat.

Ferrun watched her slack run off the side of the boat. It was moving faster than before. He thought of a dozen other things he could have said to her that would have been more helpful to her before she plunged into the water. Then the rope stopped flying off the deck. He picked it up in his hands and waited for the tug.

Ferrun didn't have to wait long, and if he hadn't been paying attention, he would have missed it. The line briefly went taut, then it went slack.

Ferrun pulled hand over hand but could barely keep up. He could imagine how furious Gesa was kicking to reach the surface. The only thing he felt he was doing at first was keeping the rope tight. Then the weight on the line got heavier. The rope required more effort to pull. Ferrun knew she was tiring out.

Seconds later, he could see her as a white splotch under the surface of the water. He pulled harder, making her features more distinct. With a final heave, her body broke the surface of the water, and she took a gasp of air, which was immediately followed by a wet cough.

Ferrun tied off the line as she worked to catch her breath. Then he went to the line that the rock was attached to. He pulled on it and felt something move at the bottom, but then the rock stopped moving as it caught on something. She hadn't made any progress despite the extra time and energy down there.

He sat on the edge of the boat and waited for her coughing and heavy breathing to stop.

She broke the silence between them first. "I think I made a little progress, but I need to go back down and finish pushing one rock out of the way."

Ferrun's face went pale as he realized what he had just done.

"What's wrong?" Gesa asked from the water.

"I think I messed it up."

Slowly Gesa asked, "What do you mean you messed it up?"

"I tried to pull up the rock, and it shifted a bit, but it got stuck again."

"It wasn't ready to be pulled!"

"I know that now," Ferrun said, feeling ashamed.

Ferrun could see her knuckles turn white as she clutched the rope ladder. She didn't look at him or accept his help as she climbed on deck.

Finally, when she'd planted her feet firmly on the deck, she said, "I don't even know why I try. As soon as I make any progress, it gets taken away from me."

"I'm sorry." Ferrun's ears were red with embarrassment. "I just thought it would be awesome if your rock was up here sooner rather than later."

Gesa bent over to pick up a big ball of rope. "It's fine. I'll just go down and risk my life...again. Like you always say, it's not the gods' fault; it's mine. It's always mine." The sound of air cut sharply into her lungs as she took a deep breath, punctuating her sentiment.

"That's not what I—"

Before he could get the rest of the words out, she had stepped off the deck of the boat.

Ferrun watched the rope slide off the deck as Gesa sank to the bottom of the ocean floor. He berated himself for doing anything with her rock without asking. The rope stopped sliding off the deck, and he picked it up, waiting for her to tug on it.

After minutes of waiting, Ferrun began to get anxious about how long she was spending down there. They had found out early on that Gesa's rock was in shallower water than Ferrun's knot had been. He wondered if he should pull her up. He wasn't comfortable with how much time had passed, but he didn't want another instance of sabotaging her work while she was making progress. However, there was also the possibility that Ferrun would be saving her life. Reaching a compromise with himself, he began to count backward from one hundred.

At forty-five seconds, he felt a tug on the rope. It was a small one, and he almost missed it while he focused on counting. He pulled the rope hand over hand, making sure to be quick while also not losing any progress by rushing. The weight was more than he'd ever lifted before. She seemed heavier, like she was pulling up a rock, or like she wasn't swimming to help him. Ferrun then realized why she wouldn't be swimming and pulled faster.

When her dead body surfaced in the ocean waves, he cursed himself for not pulling her up sooner. Gesa was now facing the uncomfortable dreams and darkness that had tortured him months ago. He heaved her body onto the boat, nearly sending a ball of rope overboard in the process.

Gesa's body was cumbersome in its inability to move of its own accord. It was essential to Ferrun that he be gentle with her though.

He didn't want her waking up with more bumps or bruises than she had when she'd first gone under.

When he laid her on the deck, lifeless and dripping wet, Ferrun realized he had no idea how to resurrect her. He didn't want to wait until the next morning for her to come back to life naturally. However, he was afraid any attempts to resurrect her could cause more problems. He hadn't learned how she had brought him back to life.

He pushed down on her chest with his hands but had no luck. He breathed into her mouth, but there was no room in her lungs for more air. The air he pushed in didn't do any good. He pressed on her stomach, trying to force her diaphragm to move her lungs. Switching between these three options and anything else that came to mind, he tried to bring her back to life. In his heart, he felt he wasn't making any progress.

As he leaned over her, trying to force air into her water-filled lungs, she coughed, covering him with salty water and mucus. She groaned and retched seawater onto the deck as Ferrun had months ago. Her eyes were far off, staring past the world and into something else. In an attempt to help, he patted her back. He didn't know if it was doing her any good, but it was nice to see life in her body again.

When she finished coughing, all she said was, "There was fire every-where—every hut was burning in the fire. I was running out of them. I was pillaging them. I was defending them. Then the fires went, and there was darkness. Absolutely nothing but darkness." She collapsed onto the deck, deep in sleep from exhaustion.

Chapter Fourteen

Gesa slept across the boat from Ferrun. He couldn't blame her. She had just returned from the dead and coughed up at least two lungfuls of air. Ferrun had made a small rope pillow for her, the same as the first night they'd met.

When she finally looked comfortable, although Ferrun suspected she was exhausted enough to sleep through anything, he began to reel in the balls of rope from the bottom of the ocean. Gesa had left two on the ocean floor in an attempt to retrieve her rock.

Ferrun pulled up Gesa's first ball with ease. It was tied tight enough that he was able to get the whole thing up in one pull. Unfortunately, the second one felt lighter, and he quickly realized that this was because the ball had become unraveled on its journey up. He pulled the rope up slowly, praying to any god willing to listen that he didn't get it caught on the ocean floor.

Soon he had the whole sopping wet unraveled rope ball on the deck. He began to wrap it back together to pass the time and add some organization to the cluttered boat that they were living on.

Halfway through the chore, Gesa began to stir on the other side of the deck. As Ferrun finished the task, she scooted over and sat next to him, leaning her head on his shoulder. Neither of them had said a word to each other since she woke up.

Ferrun tied a knot around the rope ball to keep it tight for whatever situation was in its future. Then he tied a second knot for good luck. He figured if they brought her rock on board soon, it was likely that Gesa would never need to unravel this rope.

"How did you sleep?" he finally asked.

"Would it be morose to say I slept like the dead?" she replied with a grin.

Ferrun gave her a frown at the joke, and her smile faded. Thinking back to his time being drowned, he realized that she had seen his body dead multiple times. She'd even spent a month without him. If she can make a joke, he thought, then the least he could offer is a smile. "Being dead is hard work," he said as he threw a smile back at her.

"You know what I realized on the other side, in that black void thingy you were talking about?"

"That staring into a black void with just your thoughts is no way to spend eternity." He gave a light chuckle at his joke, but when she didn't return it, he realized the time for joking was over. "What did you realize?"

Gesa made her mouth crooked as she found the right words. "I realized what I guess you were trying to explain to me. I kinda just experienced it. The void contained me and nothing and no one else. When I got back and fell asleep, I dreamed that everyone around me was just me. Then they morphed into others and became more like themselves, individuals. But I realized they were still just me but with different experiences."

"You with different experiences?" Ferrun gave her a puzzled look.

"Well, I got mad at you for messing up my rock last time by pulling it in too soon. Then I got mad when you told me it was my fault that you moved the rock."

"I never—"

"It doesn't matter either way. That's how I took it, and now I'm saying you're right. If I had all the experiences you've had in this world, I would have made the same decision. It's not your fault or my fault that things don't work out. Things just work out or they don't. I used to think that the gods run this place, that the gods decide our fate one way or another. But they're just another form of me—or, more likely, I'm another form of them."

"You think we're the gods?"

"That's what ascension is, isn't it? Entering divinity of some sort. What is time to a being like that?"

It was an idea he hadn't heard before. He didn't know how it made him feel. "You mentioned a fire." Ferrun wasn't ready to explore the idea she'd brought up.

"It's how I died. I don't like to talk about my life or death. They're both sad."

"I understand." Ferrun curbed his curiosity for her comfort.

"Thanks for pulling me up," she said, giving him a kiss on the cheek under the moonlight.

"Of course. What was I going to do? Leave you down there?"

Gesa shrugged. "If that's what me with your experiences would do, I couldn't blame you."

"How far did you get on loosening your rock?" Ferrun asked.

Gesa thought for a moment. "Maybe three-quarters of the way there. I'm close. I couldn't quite get the right grip on it, though, because the harness limits the movement of my shoulders, and I couldn't get the leverage I wanted."

"You think we can adjust how the harness holds you?" Ferrun tried to engineer a knot in his mind that would bring Gesa up by the waist instead.

"I was thinking I'd just not use it."

"Not use it?!"

"Sure," she said matter-of-factly. "I've already died once. I know what I'll face. I'll wind up above water eventually. And I'm close, so I'll probably need to face the darkness only one or two more times."

"Are you sure we're experiencing the same death?"

"I assume so. It was a big black place that swallows whatever dream you're having. It has nothing in it, and it stretches your mind and consciousness to fill it."

"That's the place."

"And it's absolute hell because you experience all of time in an instant but over and over again. And it makes you sound like a buffoon to talk about it because it's so hard to explain."

"Yes, definitely the same place. I'd never think you'd be eager to face it again."

"I guess I would just rather get my rock up here. This death and the black void thing aren't punishments for dying, just like the rock and rope aren't a punishment either. When we face it the right way, we can make progress. I think we can and should use death as a tool. Otherwise, we'll be stuck here for months or longer."

Ferrun was surprised by her new outlook. "When do you want to dive again then?"

"I'm ready when you are."

***

Without a pause they prepared for the next dive.

Gesa grabbed the two balls of rope she had taken down on the previous trips, verifying that they were both tied tight and wouldn't unravel on the way back up. With one in each hand gripped tightly, she stood at the edge of the boat. "I hope this works."

"Me too," Ferrun replied. "I won't be able to tell how far along you are." Despite her composed attitude as she stood next to the water, Ferrun could tell she wasn't eager to face death again.

"I'll be back in less than a month, so you'll be luckier than me." Her lips cracked into a faint smile.

Ferrun smiled back, knowing that he would never understand what it was like for her on the boat for the month he'd spent drowned. "Gesa, I love you. I hope you can loosen your rock to find freedom." He gave her a deep kiss, feeling the warmth of her lips. They were as warm as the noonday sun on the ocean.

"I love you too," she said when they'd finished their kiss. She turned, took a deep breath, and jumped off the side of the boat.

Ferrun leaned over and watched her figure fade from a dark, blurry spot to non-existent in the blue of the ocean water. The only thing he could do was watch her rope fly off the deck as she sank.

In only a few seconds, it stopped. Ferrun knew she'd reached the bottom. He counted the time that passed in anxious and uneven seconds, not knowing how long Gesa might be able to hold her breath. When Ferrun reached 140 seconds, he figured she would have to start swimming up. She hadn't pulled on the rope though, and even if she did, his help would likely do more harm than good. Pulling on the line in its current configuration would bring her in by her ankle like a mishooked fish.

When Ferrun counted past 200 seconds, he began pacing around the spot where she had jumped, looking into the blue water to see if her figure would reappear. His anxiety was making him count faster than he should have. At the count of 250, he figured she had run out of breath regardless of the speed he was counting.

He stopped counting, picked up her rope, and began pulling it in. It was light, and when a yard or so had landed on the deck, a blurry figure appeared under the water. An instant later, Gesa broke the surface, gasping for air.

Ferrun squatted down to offer his hand to her, and she swam over to him. With the help of the rope ladder, she quickly got on board. She lay prone on the deck, breathing heavily with her hair and linens soaked.

"I never..." Gesa gasped, "knew air..."—she took another deep breath—"could feel so..."—she quickly exhaled and inhaled deeply again—"good." Her chest moved up and down, pumping oxygen into her deprived lungs.

After a few moments of rest, she was still breathing heavily but could talk without stopping for a deep breath. "Let's try the rock. I think I got it this time."

Gesa stood up first, and Ferrun followed, if only to make sure she didn't hurt herself in her exhaustion. "It was wedged under another rock, a bigger one that wasn't tied to anything. Once I got down there without a harness, I was able to get leverage to move it easily. Honestly, I spent most of the time down there trying to swim back up. I used the tether line as a guide at first, but eventually it was quicker to just swim."

She picked up the rope that led to her rock and tugged at it. She pulled in a yard of slack and fed it back to Ferrun, who held onto it to avoid losing progress. She continued to feed him the slack, and he balled it up in neat loops.

After just over a minute, Gesa said, "I think I see something."

Ferrun took the rope he had collected so far and tied it to the deck, so a mistake wouldn't send the rock back down. The two travelers began pulling the line together. Looking over the edge of the boat, he saw a small gray blotch rising from the depths. It broke the surface. It was dark gray and smooth. The two of them heaved it onto the deck. It came up to Gesa's waist. It had a big loop knotted around it in a groove that kept it from slipping off one way or the other.

"It's like it was designed just for me," Gesa said, looking at it.

Ferrun simply stared at it and touched it. It was smooth and wet. The boat looked like it was sitting lower in the water thanks to its weight.

"I can't believe it's really here next to me," Gesa said, bubbling with excitement.

"It worked." Ferrun blinked in disbelief. He looked at her. She had tears rolling down her cheeks. He put his arms around her. "You're free to travel wherever you want! You can make it to the top of the mountain without getting stuck. If it does get stuck, you will be close enough to unstick it. This is incredible!"

"Yeah," Gesa said quietly.

"What's wrong?" Ferrun asked, pushing away from the hug to look at her face again. She was crying more than before.

"I'm free, more or less, but this means now I'm going to have to leave you to make it to the top of the mountain. And we don't even know what's up there."

Ferrun put his arms out wide and gestured to opposite horizons. "Gesa, we're in the middle of the ocean on a boat made of rope and tree trunks. I'm not going anywhere without you anytime soon. I still have rope to reel in. Eventually, we'll have to face parting ways, but who knows what's going to be at that other shore? My rock might be just sitting there waiting for me. Who knows what the gods have planned?" He didn't mention that if it were waiting on the shore, it would likely be so big that no watercraft they could build would get it across the ocean.

"Maybe."

"Come on, let's celebrate your newly won freedom. Then we'll bring in my rope and get to some dry land."

"You're right. I'm sick of rocking back and forth in my sleep," Gesa said as a small smile flitted across her face.

Chapter Fifteen

After pulling Gesa's rock up from the depths of the ocean, the two travelers were in no rush to pull in Ferrun's rope. They worked at it for a few hours every day, but their sunrise-to-sunset shifts were a thing of the past. They knew what reaching the end of the ocean voyage would mean. Neither was in a rush to split paths. The only thing that pushed them forward was their eagerness to get off the cramped boat.

In their free time, they toyed with Gesa's rock. They made idle attempts to untie the rope from it, but it was as fruitless as untying the knots on their ankles. Neither was surprised by this fact, but it was something they both felt they had to try.

After months of slow progress, the shore came into sight, and in the late morning, they pulled the boat onto the sandy beach. Ferrun's boulder was nowhere in view.

Ferrun stood barefoot in the sand, wiggling his toes. His head was so used to the pattern of the waves that it felt like he was still on the sea even though he stood on dry land.

"I can't believe I went across that thing twice!" Gesa said. "Although I'm a little less exhausted this time around."

"You're going to go across it once more to head back to the mountain." Ferrun shot her a big grin, excited about what she might find at the top.

"Yeah," she said without reflecting his excitement. She gazed at the boat. It sat tilted to one side with balls of rope overflowing from it. "I can't believe that thing got us across." She patted the wooden hull they'd sealed with sap to keep water from getting in. Ferrun's original slack was weaved between the trunks to hold the whole thing together.

"If I hadn't been on the thing this whole time, I wouldn't have thought it was even seaworthy," Ferrun said.

"I just realized. How are we going to get your rope out of the boat? It's gummed up in there. Or are you just going to start dragging this thing behind you as well?"

"I've been thinking about that for a few days. If the rope is truly impossible to break, then to clear the wood and sap, I think we should have a bonfire." A devilish grin lit up his face.

Ferrun and Gesa picked up wood and twigs and dry leaves all afternoon and set them under the boat. They unloaded Gesa's rock and rope and counted more than a dozen balls. Gesa let out enough slack that she had free reign of the beach, and she spent the first hour running up and down the shore and exploring the small forest that led up to the sand.

Ferrun, on the other hand, started looking for rocks to strike together to start a fire. He banged them together but didn't know what to expect. There were no sparks, but he figured it was because there was too much light to notice them.

"Do you have to have a special kind of rock to spark a fire?" he asked Gesa once she had worn herself out from the excitement of freedom and exploring the forest.

"I don't know. We have enough rocks here that once it's dark, we can find something that works. Besides, we're not in a rush. If it doesn't work tonight, then we can just try tomorrow."

When night came, Ferrun sat next to the kindling with his collection of rocks. He struck different combinations of stones together, keeping a careful eye out for sparks. Some rocks chipped the others. Some were too soft and became dust in his hand after his first strike. At one point, he began striking various rocks against Gesa's rock to see if he had any luck. Everything he did was fruitless.

***

The attempt to make fire dragged on for nights. During the day, Gesa would explore the forest or swim in the ocean. She was enthralled by the mobility she had from having slack and land to explore.

"Do you want to hike with me in the forest today?" Gesa asked one day as Ferrun combed the beach for a rock that might finally work.

He couldn't blame her for her excitement about the forest and the freedom her rope provided. However, he was focused on the task at hand and had so far explored only the coastline for rocks. "I'm good," he replied, looking up at her for just a second.

"Come on, it will be fun," she pleaded.

"I have to get this fire started to free my rope, and I need to find the right kind of rock to do that."

"There are rocks in the forest. Come with me. It will be fun."

Ferrun relented. "Fine."

She led him along the paths she had made through the forest, showing him all the different fascinating leaves and trees. He slowly filled his arms with rocks that he hadn't been able to find on the beach.

"You know, if we don't burn the boat, I could put a sail on it to ride back to the other side of the ocean," Gesa said when they stopped to examine some strange brown spots on a leaf.

"Oh, and let you sail into the sunset with all my rope?" Ferrun asked in a tone dripping with sarcasm.

"Well, you could come with me. And even if you didn't, you need to go back that way anyway after you find your boulder. You don't want to have to rebuild a boat, especially without my help." She gave him a flirtatious smile.

"But what if I need the slack that's in the boat?" Ferrun asked as he searched the ground for new rocks. "It just doesn't make sense. If I leave the rope here, I'd have to use slack to pick up slack as I head towards my rock. What if I run out?"

"Ferrun, you have dozens of balls of rope." Her words were strained and frustrated as she said them. "That's years of travel! You're guaranteed to find your rock before that much time passes. I don't know why you're so eager to burn the boat to free your rope."

"Because it's something holding me back," Ferrun said, reflecting her frustration. "Either I drag the boat around or I have to come back here. I don't want it to get me stuck, and I definitely don't want to get my rope stuck at a bunch of points in this whole world. What if I find a quicker way to the mountain? What if I need more slack for another boat in the future? There are a dozen things that could happen, that might happen, and I have to be prepared for them. The boat was useful for what it did. I am grateful for its service, but I need to move on."

"I guess the same goes for me. You're grateful for my service, but you need to move on!"

"No, it's not that. You've found your rock; you're free to go to the mountain. I'm holding you back like the boat is holding me back."

"Ugh! You're always thinking in terms of progress." She cracked a small branch off a dead tree. "If you're so eager to get out of here, then just rub two sticks together, you dumb ape!" She threw the branch at him and ran into the forest. Her rope trailed behind her whimsically without catching on anything.

Ferrun picked up the branch, broke two sticks off, and followed his rope back to the beach. He sat down and began rubbing the wood together as Gesa had suggested. After hours of stewing on what she had said, one of the sticks turned black in the place he continually rubbed. The black spot meant there was at least heat, and that was more progress than he'd made with the rocks. He just needed something more flammable, he thought.

After piling up some dead leaves, he rubbed his sticks over them quickly. It was exhausting, but soon enough the blackened stick began smoking, and a small ember eventually fell off. It began to catch the leaves on fire, and a small plume of smoke floated up from his leaf pile. It quickly went out, but he finally had a method that worked.

Gesa still wasn't out of the woods, and he doubted she would share in his excitement. He waited through the afternoon, hiding from the sun in the shade of their boat and improving his fire-making methods. He tied a length of vine to a stick to make a bow and drilled a divot into a flat piece of bark. Using this he was able to consistently get a fire going with some practice.

Gesa walked out of the forest at sunset. He could tell by her posture that she was still upset. She sat down next to her rope and rock, and Ferrun approached her hesitantly.

"I'm sorry for what I said." He'd said what was on his mind, but it'd hurt her, and she deserved an apology for that.

"Thanks for saying that. I'm sorry too. I've been holding you back. I've known since you had the idea of the bonfire that the rocks in this area wouldn't work. We used certain materials in the village I lived in, and I looked for them the first day. There aren't any around here."

"It's okay. I wish I'd spent more time with you instead of searching for rocks and focusing on the newest problem in front of me."

"It's who you are. I get it. It's what I love about you. It's what got us across the ocean and got me my rock."

"Thanks." Ferrun wasn't sure what to say next. "And you're not holding me back. You've got a fighting spirit. You're willing to call out the gods themselves. This forest and beach are a paradise. If staying here makes you happy, let's do it."

"Yeah, I'm great here," she said. "But it's one thing for me to want to stay here. I know the only thing you want in this world is to find your rock. And of everyone I've met in this world, you've got the tenacity to pull it off. You've got to go do it. But I'm going to stay here and enjoy this beach."

"You're not going to go back to the mountain?" Ferrun had always assumed it'd be the first thing she'd do.

"Nah," she said, poking at the sand with her feet. "I'm comfortable here. I have all the rope and slack I need. Maybe getting to the top of the mountain is just completing the first of many trials. Who's to say? I might go, and maybe the gods will give me a new challenge when I get to the top. Maybe one day I'll go, but not anytime soon."

Ferrun thought about how Merc had said there were people who camped on the side of the mountain because they were so stuck that they couldn't make any more progress. He wondered if people did that before the ascent as well and if Gesa would wind up being someone like that. "But you've made it so far!" he pleaded. "You deserve to get to the top."

"And I'll go one day," she said in an assuring tone. "One day when I'm tired of being comfortable here, in this world. But now I just want to travel and explore. This world has so much. There are different plants around every corner of that forest. The wood here is completely different from the other side of the ocean. Why? And why are there no birds or other animals here?"

"When you make it to the top of the mountain, you might learn why."

"Maybe," Gesa said with a shrug. The sun began to set above the forest behind them. "It doesn't matter what I do next. Let's burn the boat and get your rope free. I trust you got the sticks to work?"

"Yeah," Ferrun said, a little disheartened.

With an excited smile, she said, "Come on, then, let's have a bonfire!"

Chapter Sixteen

Ferrun showed her his method for consistently starting a fire. Even with the two of them and the improved technique, it was a slow process. Once a fire was burning, it was hard to get all the wood to burn at the same time. One side of the boat would start smoking, so they'd switch to the other, but then the first side would blow out. Eventually, the majority of it caught, and even the ocean's breeze couldn't put it out.

Gesa and Ferrun sat in each other's arms on a rope seat they made after the boat had caught fire. It was spectacular. The sap Ferrun had suggested for waterproofing the hull was more flammable than the wood, and soon the entire thing was roaring. The seawater made the logs crackle and pop, launching sparks into the air like fireworks every so often. The blaze put off so much heat that the two had to move their couch back.

"If the gods weren't watching us cross the ocean, then this fire should be bright enough to get their attention," Ferrun said.

"I have a feeling they never stopped watching you." The fire lit up an endearing smile on Gesa's lips.

Ferrun sat upright on their rope cushion. "Can I say something?"

"You just did," Gesa said as the dancing light revealed her smirk.

"Merc told me that people just kind of get stuck here in this world. Their rope gets stuck and they stop, or they get bored and stop making progress. I couldn't fathom it. But now that I've been here a while, I get it. I don't like it, but I get it." Ferrun rubbed the back of his neck as he thought of how to phrase the next words he wanted to say. "I...I don't want the same thing to happen to you. Hell, you're the last person in this world who has an excuse to get stuck. I know you're not eager to make a beeline to the mountain, and that's fine. It's your afterlife, and you can spend it how you want. But I would be remiss if I just let you quit moving after you've accomplished so much." He gestured to where her rock lay on the beach.

"No, you're right. I was thinking about it while we were trying to get the fire to start. I was thinking about how once you light one fire, you can use it to easily create a second one. Then you have two fires. That doesn't work with food or sticks or water. There are only a few things you can duplicate without taking away from the first. And I want to work on that."

"Work on what?" Ferrun said with a puzzled look.

"I want to work on sharing your idea. I want to explore this place and map it out. Maybe a map would help others find their way to the mountain."

"That's a noble goal. Who knows how big this place is?"

"I have an eternity to do it. Maybe I'll be the last one up the mountain, be a genuine guide for people, unlike what I did in my life."

"I hope not," Ferrun said, concerned.

"Anyway, this whole 'follow your rope back to the rock' idea—it's one of those things I could give others without taking anything away from myself. And I'd be proof it works!" Her tone and face were both excited, and the fire exaggerated the whole expression.

"That would be amazing." Ferrun was reminded of his old friend Teekola. "People just laughed at me when they saw me traveling away from the mountain and picking up my rope. But if you showed them, you'd have proof! Man, I wish I could see that happen."

"And, honestly, I'd be doing it for you, because of you. You're the one who gave me this idea. Without your help, I'd be on the other beach still pulling at my rope."

"You'd have figured something out eventually."

"Maybe! Or maybe I'd be another one of those people stuck in one spot for eternity. I'm here with my rock because you shared your fire with me. But it was your fire first. I'd feel bad beating you to the top of the mountain."

"Oh, don't worry about that." It was something Ferrun had never considered a problem. "I'll likely never make it to the top with the size my boulder is. Maybe my whole purpose is to be stuck here—stuck so I'd get the idea and spread it to others so they can be free."

"I don't think so, Ferrun. I spent a lot of time with you on that boat. You're not the kind of person who stays stuck for long." The firelight was caught in her eyes and danced around her pupils.

Ferrun kissed her, and her lips and body warmed him more than the bonfire across the beach ever could. It was a warmth that would stay with him however far he traveled in this world.

***

Ferrun stood at the curb, waiting for the bus. The podcast he was listening to droned on about a murder that had happened years ago and still wasn't solved. But the ball rang through his ear, cutting the podcaster off every time it bounced and letting out a high-pitched cry.

The bus came around the corner and approached the group of people. Ferrun pulled his bus pass out of his pocket and nervously fiddled with it in his hand.

His attention was on the girl and her bouncing ball. He heard the air brakes of the bus engage, and he wanted to grab the girl to keep her from even bouncing the ball in the street, but his body was in its usual paralyzed state.

He pushed against it, wanting to be free to run through this dream and save everyone the heartache of watching poor Ally/Amy/Anny being hit by the bus. But the paralysis fought back, and he couldn't move.

The ball bounced oddly on the sidewalk. It bounced into the street. Ferrun was focused on it, but somehow the scene still felt like he was noticing the ball for the first time.

Ally/Amy/Anny realized it immediately and chased after the ball. Ferrun's body moved as he chased after the girl. He'd fought it for so long that moving now felt motionless.

With a long step, he was in the street and had caught up with the girl. He pushed her back to the curb with both hands. He wished he could have done it gentler, he wished he wasn't just shoving her onto the sidewalk, but he didn't have much time.

She fell backward, tripping over the curb and scraping her elbows and knees. Her mother was there, trying to decipher what was going on. But that was the last thing Ferrun saw.

His head hit the front of the bus, and the world went black.

***

Ferrun sat up, jolted awake by the adrenaline that still rushed through his system from the dream. Sitting up on the rope pallet, he saw the embers of the bonfire glowing orange in the dark.

"You all right?" Gesa asked.

"Yeah, I'm fine," Ferrun said after taking a deep breath.

He lay back down, and Gesa snuggled up next to him. He stared up at the stars, glad that Ally/Amy/Anny was safe, short of some scrapes.

III

Desert

Chapter Seventeen

The sun heated Ferrun's back as he pulled his balls of rope across the sand. His feet were covered in fresh burns, and while he knew they'd heal in the morning, every step seared his soles. He looped more of the hot rope onto the small ball in his hand. Out of habit, he licked his cracked lips, but it felt like rubbing two sheets of sandpaper against each other.

To check the time, he put his hand in front of the sun so he could look up into the bright sky. The sun was reaching its peak, and Ferrun didn't know how many more steps were left in him. Despite waking up every morning rehydrated and healed, he was collecting rope at half his normal speed. As he pulled the next yard in, the hot rope slipped from his tired fingers.

Ferrun bent over to pick it up, and as he did his knees buckled. His face landed on the sand, pushing dust into his already dry mouth. He used all the strength in his arms to push himself up, but it wasn't enough. Once again, the heat of the desert had worn him down before the afternoon.

His breaths were labored as the desert breeze blew sand on top of him, and he wondered if one day he would wake up buried in a dune. But that was his last thought before his lungs became too tired to function. His mind drifted off into a dream from his past life.

During the day, Ferrun wanted to face these dreams with indifference. After all, they always disappeared in the morning. He dreamed he was struggling to design that construction material before his annual review deadline. But when he was in the dream, he hated watching the experiment fail over and over again no matter what he tried. In the moment of the dream, it felt like it lasted forever. He wanted to take some action to stop it like he had with the girl and the bus, but whenever he realized what he needed to do differently, he never could. Eventually the experiment would fail, and the darkness of the void would swallow him up, stretching his mind in ways it wasn't supposed to go.

Now the void shrank, and he was resurrected by the early sunlight of dawn. Instead of his mouth being full of water, he had sand on his tongue and in his teeth. He fought the urge to spit the grit out because it would be a waste of the limited moisture he had for the day.

The sun peeked above the horizon. He noticed a speck in the distance but dismissed it as a mirage in the shimmering sand. Taking advantage of his morning energy, he dusted himself off and began to collect his rope and move across the desert.

The sand, which started cool from the night, quickly warmed as the sun rose into the sky. Soon each step agonized his newly blistered feet. The wind was dry and hot, and it felt like he was walking through an oven. Before the sun was a quarter of the way through the sky, Ferrun was miserable. Despite this, he continued to collect his rope.

His rope ball grew slower than it had in the forest. He'd estimated at least two months had passed since he and Gesa parted ways on the beach, and he had only a ball and a half to show for it. He was painfully aware that he'd collected most of that rope while he traipsed through the small beachside forest.

The desert had immediately cut his progress in half. He wasn't able to work the whole day without dying of heat exhaustion. At first, he didn't know what was happening. He woke up from the dreams, assuming he'd fallen asleep for the night. But his slow plodding journey across the desert eventually revealed what was really happening.

Ferrun arrived at the speck as the sun neared its peak. It was a man passed out in the sand. This man was the first person Ferrun had seen since leaving Gesa. His skin was lobster red and nearly matched the hair on his head. A thin layer of sand lay on top of his white linens. Ferrun was on his last reserves of energy, and he would soon be joining this man, face down on the sand.

Thinking about the massive number of rope balls he had behind him, he decided to build an enclosure to shade himself and the man in their deaths. He ended his hiking through the sand and began to roll his balls around the man. He made a domelike structure with a small gap to use as a door. As he reached up to complete the top of the dome, his legs gave out, and he fell to the ground. He was partly shaded by the roof, but there was still a hole in it where sun leaked through as his eyes became heavy and he drifted into dreams of his past life.

More experiments failed, and his grant was running out of money. He pushed to try new things, but he was stuck in the memories of the past and how they failed to accomplish anything. The experiments ended with an awful explosion, and it wrapped him into the dark void. His mind was stretched to the boundaries of the void, pulled as thin as a spider's web. But after an eternity, the void dissolved.

Ferrun sat up, staring across the small rope dome at the man he'd found in the desert. The man looked at Ferrun but seemed more surprised by the shelter above his head.

"What is this?" he asked in confusion.

"Rope," Ferrun replied as he evaluated the craftsmanship of the structure. There were gaps between the balls of rope, and small shafts of morning light jutted in. It wasn't perfect, but it shaded them. He couldn't believe he'd built it in the heat of the midday sun.

"Rope? Where did you get so much?" Envy seeped into the man's eyes.

"I made the mistake of asking for my rope to be attached to the biggest rock they had," Ferrun said, rubbing the back of his neck.

"That does sound like a mistake. Why didn't you pick a normal-sized one?"

"I'm still working out an answer to that one."

The two men spent the morning in the shade. The man said his name was Gray, and he'd only ever seen the desert since his arrival. He was fascinated by Ferrun's journey and questioned every aspect of his adventure, from where he'd started to the voyage across the sea, to drowning to untie his rope, and to the details of Gesa and Teekola supporting his idea. Gray scoffed at the idea of going back to his rock and the idea that anyone would buy it as a good idea. When Ferrun got to the beginnings of his travels in the desert, Gray happily chimed in.

"I used to think the days were short," Gray said. "I'd drag my rock for about half the day, then I'd pass out. I didn't even realize I was dying. Since day one, my days just ended in the middle, and I'd face hallucinations of my past. Then I'd see the thing you call a dark void. I thought I was in my own personal hell. You're the first person I've met, but I figured I wasn't alone, though, since I'd come across a few rocks with rope around them.

"Eventually, I found a pool of water in the middle of the desert. I rested there, and that's when I realized there were full days and I was just dying midway through." He chuckled a deep laugh. "I spent a few days there recovering. Then I started on again. But I'm not making much progress. I'm still dehydrating since I don't have a way to hold the water I found. How did you last so much longer than me?"

"I suspect it's because I'm merely picking up my rope, while you're pulling yours along. Does it ever get stuck?"

"No. How could it? There's just sand all over the place."

Ferrun knew how far into the desert they were, and it gave him the idea that Gray's rope might be quite short. If he turned around today, he could be free from pulling that rock in a few months. Ferrun realized he could save the man time and torture if he could get the skeptic to turn back. "How far away is the oasis you mentioned?"

"It's been a few days," the man said as he licked his parched lips. The rope shelter provided the men shade, but the air was still dry, and they were still sweating. "You think we could survive all day in this rope shelter?"

Ferrun rubbed the back of his hand, thinking. "Maybe. But we'd be stuck, unable to move. Could you take us back to the water?"

"Having all this rope is pretty nifty," he said, not answering Ferrun's question. He eyed the rope like a prowling cat. "I can't make progress at the oasis. Not that I know which way progress is anymore. I'm walking in the opposite direction of my rock, which makes sense. But now you say the mountain is on the other side of some ocean. How am I supposed to get across that?" He shook his head in frustration. "Plus, you claim you're from the same direction as my rock. And I don't know why the gods would put my rock on this path. I should be walking away from my rock like everyone else you've met."

"If it's not getting stuck, then it's probably just in the desert. You're so close to your rock though. It'd take no time for you to get there. And it'd save you so much time in the long run."

"Long run?" the man scoffed. "I think you need to get a grip on what eternity means." He made to crawl out through the small doorway of the rope hut.

"Wait! Just lead me to where the oasis is. Then you can do whatever you want." Ferrun was frantically stalling to keep the man from heading on his way. He wanted to show Gray how easy picking up rope could be and thought maybe the guy would be free enough to reach the top of the mountain before anyone else. "I know you don't want to backtrack on your rope. I'm not eager to be letting out slack to move away from my goal either. But it's so hot and dry. We need some water."

Gray was on his hands and knees, crawling for the door. He looked back across the small rope hut at Ferrun, then he crawled the rest of the way out of the shelter. "Come on, then. I think we've waited long enough that we might get to sleep tonight. It looks like it's past midday."

Ferrun scooted out the small door in excitement. He'd succeeded in convincing the skeptic to give picking up rope a shot. He was hopeful he'd be able to show Gray how much more freeing it was to pick up a rope instead of dragging a boulder along.

Chapter Eighteen

G ray slowly pulled in his rope, wrapping it in disorganized balls, poorly mimicking the pattern Ferrun had shown him. "Do you think it's time to stop?" The two men were dehydrated, and this was the first thing either had said since late afternoon.

Parched, Ferrun took a minute to get his throat to reply. "Are you too tired to continue?"

Gray gave an ambiguous shrug, which Ferrun had quit trying to encourage meaning out of days ago. Ferrun suspected continuing would lead to more resistance from him.

The two men began to set up camp. They used Ferrun's dozens of rope balls stacked in circles to build a small hut. Ferrun packed balls around the majority of the first layer of the shelter until his work connected with the few balls Gray had put in place. The pattern repeated, shrinking layer by layer, until they had a small dome of rope balls.

Crawling inside, Ferrun found the shade refreshing. The sand still burned his shins and knees, but he knew it would keep them warm as the night cooled everything down.

"How much further do you think we have?" Ferrun asked.

"Can't be much further but could be more. I'm not much of a navigator," Gray said as he lay on his back to go to sleep.

Ferrun had never met anyone else in this world who went to bed so quickly after a day of walking. Even accounting for the heat of the day and the weight of the man's rope, Ferrun was surprised by how quickly Gray settled down for the night.

"What did you do in your life?" Ferrun said, still not ready to sleep.

"Huh?" Gray was still lying on his back with his eyes closed.

"Before this. Do you remember what you did?"

"It's vague," Gray said, looking up at the ceiling of rope balls. "I did research."

"Me too," Ferrun said, excited. "What kind of research?"

"Exobiology." Grey glanced over at him. "The study of alien life," he added as though he didn't think Ferrun would recognize the prefix.

"You found aliens?"

"Or they found us. Still not sure. I just know whatever I was studying went bad."

"I know how that goes," Ferrun said, remembering dreams and memories where he'd messed up his own experiment or didn't get the funding he needed.

"No, you don't."

"It's part of the job. Sometimes things don't go right. But we're searching for truth, not trying to feed our egos."

"Did whatever you study ever break out of its cage, project horrific hallucinogenic visions into your mind, then devour you limb by limb?"

"No," Ferrun said, trying to gauge if he should laugh or be concerned.

"Then I guess you don't know how that goes." Gray rolled over, turning his back to Ferrun.

Unsure of what he could say, Ferrun quietly made a pallet to sleep on.

***

Gray slept through most of the morning. Without much to do, Ferrun tied knots in his rope and wished there was a twig around so he could try to master the trick Teekola did with twirling it around his fingers. He was beginning to wonder if he should be offended by Gray's sleeping patterns. It was making it difficult for him to convince the man to continue following his rope past the oasis, which was the whole point of letting out slack to travel with the man.

Midday arrived, and the sun shined straight through the gap at the top of the hut. Gray got up from his slumber at that point, ready to get going. They'd die in the heat if they left before midday, but Ferrun wasn't convinced that Gray was really sleeping that many hours.

The two men sweated and walked in silence. They had shared all the stories they had the first few days. After that, Ferrun had reached the point of talking to hear himself speak. He didn't like wasting the moisture and so kept quiet more often than not.

As the afternoon came to a close and dusk began, Ferrun asked, "What do you think about going the rest of the way to get to your rock?"

Gray gave a small shrug as he looped a bit of rope in his hand.

"I bet you wouldn't have much. If your rock isn't getting stuck on anything, it's likely still in the desert. I've been to the edge of this place, and it's not too far away." Ferrun thought of the long distance he'd traveled in search of his rock.

"Maybe," Gray said nonchalantly, "but if it's not stuck on anything, what reason do I have to go back?"

"Well, it's not stuck yet, but it's not just desert from here to the mountain."

Gray shrugged. It wasn't a blatant disagreement, which is what made it so hard for Ferrun to continue the conversation.

"I think maybe it's time to stop for today," Gray said. The sun had dipped behind the horizon, but they could still see by the light of the moon.

Ferrun decided to disagree with him since Gray was so comfortable doing it. "I think we can go a little further. Besides, who knows how close the oasis might be?"

Gray's only response was a heavy sigh as he continued his lethargic wrapping of rope.

They crested two more dunes before Ferrun asked, "Is that the oasis?!" His voice was hoarse but full of excitement.

"Suppose so," Gray said as he sat down on the top of the dune, exhausted.

"We could make it there tonight. Your rope leads right to it."

"Maybe. Or we could sleep here for the night and get to it in the morning."

Unexcited about Gray's suggestion, Ferrun continued walking. As he wandered his way down the steep side of the dune, he noticed Gray was still following him. In only a few minutes, they were at the oasis with cool grass beneath their toes.

"Think we need to build a hut?" Ferrun asked as he rubbed his hand in the grass. He'd taken vegetation for granted the whole time he'd traveled through the forest.

Gray shrugged and wandered towards the water. Ferrun lay down, and the comfort of the grass compared to the hard sand carried him off to sleep quickly.

***

Ferrun woke up knowing something wasn't quite right. Exhausted, he had slept deeply through the night, but now it was early morning, and he felt pins and needles in his arms from the way he had lain. He tried to roll over to ease the sensation, but he found he couldn't move. His drowsiness quickly left him as he realized he was stuck in one position and bound by rope. He began to cry out for Gray's help, but "*mrrt mrr mrll*" was the only thing he could get out. His mouth was full of rope.

Gray soon loomed over him as he struggled against the rope. "I don't know what you're trying to do to me, but I'm catching on. You dragged me through the entire desert back to this oasis. And now we finally get here only to find it empty." His eyes were focused on something far in the distance. "I don't know what you did to get so much rope, but you're obviously up to something. Maybe you want to distract everyone you meet so you can claim whatever is on top of that mountain for yourself. Or maybe you're a demon trying to keep me locked in this hell forever. Either way, I haven't trusted you since I first heard your extravagant tale. I would have just told you to follow my rope to get to this place, but I didn't trust you with it. Gods only know what trickery you can do with it."

Ferrun looked at the man above him with wide eyes. Unable to speak, he just looked around in horror. He knew he couldn't die in this world, but he wasn't sure what Gray might do. The man had already done more than he thought anyone in this afterlife ever would. "*Mrr mrdn't mrrrt*," he mumbled.

"Come look at what you've done to the oasis." Gray grabbed a length of Ferrun's binding and dragged him across the grassy land.

The sand beneath the grass gritted against the skin on Ferrun's legs and feet. For a man who fell asleep quickly and wanted to make camp before sunset, Gray had no lack of strength. Gray quit dragging him and roughly rotated Ferrun to face the middle of the oasis.

A vast tan pit lay in front of them. The sand was darker than what they had traveled across, especially towards the bottom, but there was no water in it like Ferrun had expected.

"It was full when I left. You think it just all evaporated as soon as I decided to come back? You were behind this. I know it." Gray shot him a cruel look. "You want me to go back to my rock, and I'm not sure why, but I'm done listening to your crazy ideas. I barely believed your story to begin with. But I'm not just going to ignore you and move on like these other people you've fooled. I'm going to do the rest of this world a favor and tie you up real tight so you can't distract anyone else. I wonder if that Teeko guy or the girl you mentioned ever truly reached their rock. Or if they were just stories you told others to convince them to follow your misguided ways." He gave a shrug indicating the answer wouldn't change his plans.

Ferrun stared at the pit in the sand as he heard Gray walk away. He wondered if the desert sun had made Gray crazy, and he didn't like the thought of the same happening to him. The world wouldn't let them die, but Ferrun had already lost his mind at the bottom of the sea once, and he wasn't looking forward to going through that again.

Ferrun could only wiggle around as he heard Gray moving behind him. Every time he rotated enough to get a glimpse of his captor, Gray would come over and turn him forcefully back towards the empty pit. As the sun rose in the sky, the dark brown sand at the bottom of the pit turned a light tan. Ferrun sweated through the morning, but as the sun rose, his sweating stopped altogether. The only information he could glean from his short glimpses at Gray's work was that he was doing something elaborate with Ferrun's rope.

The sun began to fall from the sky, and Ferrun felt the exhaustion of the heat. He knew he had to get some moisture to survive the day. There was no water in the pit where the oasis was supposed to be, and the sand below him was bone dry, so he wouldn't find any help there. The only thing within reach with any moisture was the grass that his face was pressed against.

In desperation, he took a bite of some. It wasn't as refreshing as a sip of water, and he wasn't even sure if it would work. He hadn't needed to eat anything in this world for so long that the sensation of chewing felt strange. He bit off a little more grass, and while he didn't feel renewed, it was something he could do to defy Gray, who was still working behind him.

Soon the afternoon passed, and Ferrun's stomach felt sick from eating grass. Behind him Gray was silent, and the last thing he'd said had been a while ago. Ferrun wasn't sure if that was because he had completed the project or had died in the process. He slowly wiggled around to see the man before the sun disappeared from the sky.

Gray lay on the ground, asleep or dead. Ferrun wasn't sure. What he was sure of was that Gray had made a massive knot between all the rope balls that Ferrun had collected. It wasn't the unintentional knotting of carelessness but instead the deliberate, malicious knots of a madman. If Ferrun ever got free from the bonds that held him, ones made from his own rope, he would have to spend a long time unknotting the mess that Gray had made.

Chapter Nineteen

F errun lay crooked in the grass of the desert, his face resting against the shortened blades of grass he'd eaten. The rope, his rope, in front of him was horrifically knotted, and he was utterly unsure of what to do about it. All he could do was stare at the mess Gray had made of the rope and wiggle against his bonded wrists and ankles. He was eventually exhausted enough that he couldn't stay awake, and he fell into a fitful sleep dreaming of betrayals by his friends and family in his previous life.

Ferrun was jarred awake by Gray pulling on his rope. The man was tightening the already restrictive bonds and removing any progress Ferrun had made in the night. When he was finished, the man took a tight hold of the rope and rolled Ferrun over to face him.

"You saw what I've done?" Gray asked.

Ferrun wanted to spit at the man who looked down at him. Unfortunately, with the rope running across his mouth, the only thing he could do was glower in the man's general direction.

"I hope you're stuck here for eternity. If that oasis were full, then I'd throw you into the bottom of it, hoping you'd drown. Eternity should be plenty of time for you to atone for all the people you've tricked with your stories about turning around and getting your rock." Gray rolled Ferrun over so he was face down in the sand, and pulled tightly on the knots. "Now if you don't mind, I'm going to leave you so I can start making up some of the progress I've lost by humoring you."

After he'd heard Gray's footsteps disappear, Ferrun began wiggling against his restraints. His legs and arms were asleep, and his shoulder blades and hips were sore from being pulled against the way they were supposed to go. Gray had pulled both his legs and arms behind his back and tied them together, making it impossible for Ferrun to crawl or wiggle. He merely wobbled back and forth, pulling his hands against the bonds.

The sun rose high into the sky as he struggled, and the sand beneath him grew warm by the sun's heat. He ran out of sweat and knew that it was midday. The bonds weren't getting any looser despite his struggle against them. The sun had drained his body of energy and moisture. He knew he'd pass out or die soon if he didn't get some liquid into him. He felt hopeless and didn't see the point of trying to stay alive. More hours awake meant more hours of pointlessly struggling against his bonds. He decided it was better to be alive and bound than dead and facing the uncomfortable nightmares ending in the black void.

Ferrun began to munch on the grass. He bit into the bitter turf and ground it as best he could with his back teeth. It didn't give him much energy, but he knew from the day before that it would be enough moisture to survive. Despite spending an afternoon fighting his bonds, the struggle bore no fruit. They were just as tight as they'd been at the start of the day.

***

The sun dipped below the horizon as Ferrun wiggled in the sand. Soon the cool night air was blowing around him. He was exhausted from the heat and his day of struggling against the rope. Unfortunately, his body was in too uncomfortable a position to sleep. As he lay on his stomach in the dark of the night, he heard liquid dripping in the distance. It reminded him of rainwater running off trees and into a puddle, but there wasn't a cloud in the sky. The faint dripping sound combined with the uncomfortable position kept Ferrun from sleeping through the night.

After a whole night of struggling against his ropes, Ferrun figured out how to move himself around with the momentum of his body. It was a slow process, and occasionally a tuft of grass would get in his way. He didn't care about the speed because as the sun rose in the sky, he was able to move. He wouldn't be able to make it to the top of the mountain this way, but he was able to move towards the dripping sound. The sound got fainter as the day progressed, but he kept trying to make progress towards it.

Ferrun reached the edge of the pit that Gray had claimed used to hold the oasis water. Looking down the sloped sides, he saw a small pool of water at the bottom. There wasn't much water in it, but considering it was empty the last time he'd seen it, he was stunned.

Looking over the edge, he debated whether he should roll himself down into the pit. It looked like a flattened cone, and the tumble would be uncomfortable but survivable. He was still sweating, but he knew from experience that he would soon be out of sweat. His stomach was upset from the copious amounts of grass he had to eat to stay hydrated, so he made his decision. Using his bound arms and legs, he shifted his weight back and forth.

Ferrun built up enough momentum to push himself over the edge of the pit. Once he was over the edge, gravity and the slope of the pit took care of the rest. His body flopped end over end. Every rotation of his body crushed his awkwardly placed arms and legs and pounded his exposed stomach. The rolling didn't help his stomachache either, and his guts felt like they were in a washing machine. Then it came to an end. He landed face first in the puddle of water.

The chill of the water slapped his dry face. Whatever fed the puddle was protected from the heat of the sun. Unfortunately, he was face first in the water. Ferrun was aware of the outcome of having his head underwater for long periods and didn't want to experience it again. He forced himself to roll over as best he could. Landing on his side, he was able to lift his head out of the water but felt the uncomfortable sensation of water rushing into his nose.

Ferrun dipped his head back into the puddle to get a drink, and the liquid felt refreshing to his lips. He kept drinking until he was full. As he held his head out of the water, he noticed that the dripping sound had stopped.

Ferrun rocked himself until he was rotated enough to avoid falling into the water. He used his arms and legs behind him to keep himself from rolling farther into the pit and balanced himself into a position where he was able to sleep. It wasn't the most comfortable position, but after a night of not sleeping and a day of rocking himself across the oasis, he slept deep and dreamlessly.

Ferrun slept away the rest of the morning and the beginning of the afternoon near the shallow pool of water. By afternoon, it was too hot for him to sleep without shade, and the sun's heat had ruined the refreshing coolness of the water. The lukewarm water wasn't appetizing, but the sun's heat made him wiggle around for another drink. As he moved, he noticed that his wet bonds felt tighter than they had before.

The more he moved against them to investigate, the tighter the wet bonds became. His heart sank as he realized that his attempt to get water had jeopardized his chances of untying himself. Now his only chance to escape was to have someone wander by and set him free. Even with all of eternity, Ferrun felt that it wasn't likely to happen.

As the afternoon sun beat down on him, he was grateful that he had water. The sun dried his wet linens and his tightened bonds. Slowly the water receded away. By the time the wall of the pit cast shade over Ferrun, he was no longer at the water's edge. He merely sat on a moist bed of sand. The bonds around his wrists and ankles had dried out, and the rope felt stiffer than before. It seemed that the heat of the day and the change in moisture had also made the bonds a little looser than they were initially. He wiggled against them, but his hands were still stuck.

As he fought against his dried-out rope in the shade of the pit, he heard the dripping begin again. This time it wasn't a single drop. Instead, it sounded like a dozen drops dripping at random intervals. He looked to the puddle in the dim evening sun and saw that the water level was growing again. The water was a foot away but seemed to be recovering from the day's evaporation, and it slowly crept towards him. He was glad for the liquid's proximity because the afternoon sun had made him thirsty.

He wiggled against his bonds, feeling a small gap between his wrist and the rope. He could almost fit his hand through, but his thumb blocked the way. The water continued to rise, and he could swear the dripping was getting faster. He looked at the waterline, and it was almost at him. He rolled away from it to keep his bonds from getting wet and tight again. Lying on his side facing the water, his hands were safe. However, his face would be under the water shortly. He dug his hands and feet into the slope of the pit, but he knew he wouldn't be able to roll up the side to escape.

Ferrun pulled hard against the bonds, but his hand was still too fat to fit through the tiny opening that was there. He kicked to stretch the rope in strange ways, but this didn't bring him any success.

The water was beginning to reach his nose, and his struggling was kicking up loose sand that became grit in his mouth. He felt the sand at his hands absorbing moisture, and he knew the rope would soon become wet as well.

Ferrun took a deep breath to brace himself for what he had to do. His left hand grabbed the one that was too fat to fit through the gap. He pressed his right thumb towards his palm as hard as he could. He didn't want to do it, but he also didn't want to drown in the desert. He pushed against his right thumb with all of his strength and let out a howl when a bone in his thumb snapped. He pulled his right hand against the rope again. With his thumb broken, he was able to slip it out.

Ferrun pulled the bonds off his other hand. He had some trouble with them since he wasn't able to use his thumb. By the time his face was under the water, he'd freed both hands. With two free hands, he was able to sit up in the water.

His feet landed in the growing pool, and the bonds on them absorbed the moisture. Since they were wet and would tighten, Ferrun made sure not to move his feet more than he had to. He knew he wouldn't be able to swim against the water with his feet tied, so he went to work to untie them. Every time he forgot his thumb was broken, the searing pain reminded him, and the bruise that was growing there began to make his right fingers hurt as they moved.

The wet rope slipped off his feet as the water reached his waist. Once his feet were free, he scrambled up the side of the pit, using his good hand to help him keep balance.

Soon he sat safely on a grassy mound at the edge of the oasis pool. Ferrun listened to the water drip as it filled the pit. He held his throbbing thumb against his chest, glad to be free of the bonds. He fell back exhausted on the grass of the oasis and fell asleep.

***

Ferrun looked at the pair of men sitting at the table. They were snacking on some chips, waiting for their meal. Ferrun sat in the booth next to them and was able to hear their conversation as clear as if he were a part of it.

"Did you hear they developed that material Ferrun was working on?" The man had a familiar long face, but his hair was shorter than Ferrun expected. It was almost to his scalp on the sides, but the top was long and voluminous.

"Yeah," the older man sitting across from him said. "But I haven't read the paper yet."

"You should. It'd be interesting since you read some of Ferrun's notes."

"I think I still have them somewhere, on an old hard drive."

"Did he publish anything about it?" Jeremy asked. The man's name finally came back to Ferrun. "It'd be interesting if we could get his name on the patent or at least get him acknowledged in some way."

"I don't think he did," Dr. Long said. "It was a real sore point in our annual reviews. I wish I hadn't pushed him so hard."

"He always thought you were supportive of the project."

"Maybe he would have shown up to work on time if I had been."

"Don't say that."

Their server, a motherly figure with a tattoo on her arm of an old-fashioned spinning wheel, approached with their food. She placed down a burger and some fried chicken while Jeremy asked for a refill on his beer.

"They could have used the material a few years ago." Jeremy continued to bring up pasts that couldn't be changed. "When all those shortages hit. This kind of development could have changed things."

"Ferrun would have had to get it done." The old man spoke of a past Ferrun never knew. "Three years after his death."

"He might have figured it out by then," Jeremy said optimistically.

"Maybe. Assuming we didn't let him go before then. He wasn't publishing anything."

"His mind was focused on the project. In all the years I knew him, he wasn't one to back down from a problem he started."

"He knew how to pick them though."

"How's that kid doing anyway?"

The old man shrugged. "Last I heard, the parents were still avoiding talking about it publicly. Probably avoided telling her as well."

"She's got to be out of high school by now. She's figured it out by now."

The old man shook his head as if to Etch-A-Sketch the memory away. "I don't think I'd want to know what my life cost."

The conversation faded, and Ferrun sat in his booth, looking around the familiar bar. They talked about research Ferrun didn't understand because he hadn't kept up with the trends. They talked about people he'd never met because they'd been born too recently. The pool table in the back caught his attention, and it looked well worn. The server returned with Jeremy's beer, and she handed Ferrun a menu.

"What can I get you?" she asked.

Ferrun looked down at the menu. The name of the bar was different, and the logo had a black eight ball on the cover. He stared at it, knowing he wanted something without grass. He opened the menu, and instead of seeing a list of dishes to order, he saw a darkness unleash and swallow him whole.

Chapter Twenty

F errun woke up shivering in the dim light of morning. The cool night air blew past him, and the sand no longer stored the heat of the day. He paced around the edge of the oasis to warm up but couldn't go far with his ankle tied to the mess Gray had made.

The oasis had filled to its halfway point in the night. It was a big pool, and Ferrun didn't doubt that he would have drowned and been stuck underwater if he hadn't freed himself the night before. Thankfully the new morning healed his thumb, and full use of it returned. After taking a refreshing sip of water from the pool, he went to his rope.

The chaos that Gray had caused with the rope was more than Ferrun thought anyone could do. Ferrun had organized it so thoroughly, and it used to be easy to unroll and reroll anytime he needed it. Gray had combined all of Ferrun's dozens of rope balls into a massive knot. He could see some of the balls still intact with inner bits of rope pulled to the outside and knotted to other strands of rope. He didn't know where to start, and he eventually returned to the pool of water.

It would be a long time until the knotted mess of slack would be able to roll anywhere. Sitting at the edge of the half-full pit, he kicked his feet over the side. Alone in the heat of the midday sun, Ferrun didn't know what he was going to do.

***

Ferrun wasted the heat of the afternoon too deflated to begin untangling the knot Gray had made. By dusk he summoned the courage to face it. Under the dim light of the setting sun, he followed his rope over to the massive knot ball and began to work at it.

Soon he stood in darkness, only able to use his hands to feel the rope. The moon was a sliver in the sky and shed no light on the situation. Slowly and carefully, he fed the rope through itself to unknot the mess.

Ferrun quickly found tricks that Gray had hidden in the rope. The rope would come out of one end, then loop around to the other, causing Ferrun to walk all the way around the knot to get to a minor knot that was keeping him from loosening the strand he was working on.

As the night continued on, Ferrun felt he was amassing a large pile of slack. The progress energized him. He even dreamed he would untie the knot in a day or two since Gray hadn't spent more than a day tying it together.

As the sun crept above the horizon, light came back into Ferrun's world. Before him lay a knot of rope that seemed just as large as the one he'd seen at the beginning of the night. It was still taller than him. It was still wider than him. The only sign that his night hadn't been a waste was the small loop of slack that sat in a ring around the mess.

Even that slack was a mess. Ferrun had no illusions about that. The small upside was that it wasn't a knotted mess like the behemoth in front of him. He looked at all of his rope and sighed. Despite being tired from the night, he slogged on.

Being able to see the knot now, Ferrun expected to be better at untying it. Unfortunately, he found himself tracing the wrong strands of rope with his eyes and making a mess of the progress he'd made in the night. The sun was only a few hours into the sky when he gave up.

Stepping back, he looked at the ring of rope around the knot and thought it might be smaller than when it was at the beginning of the day. Despite this, he began looping it into his familiar rope ball pattern to keep it organized and from getting knotted up more.

Before midday Ferrun had a small ball of rope. He suspected it was a little shy of one month of travel. Doing some quick math, he realized that he had been dragging more than two dozen balls of rope behind him before Gray had made a mess of things. It was enough to build a small shelter after all. He hopelessly lay back in the sand of the oasis, realizing he'd be at this project for almost a month at this rate.

Discouraged by the math, he bathed in the oasis, hoping to refresh himself. He also drank some of the pool's water to recover from the heat of the early sun. Another upside of the work he'd put in was that he now had enough slack to reach a tree in the oasis. He slumped under it and slept the afternoon away.

When the sun began to disappear from the sky, Ferrun slowly woke up from his sleep. He groggily walked over to his knot of rope. Unable to see the whole ball in the dim light of the moon, he felt around the knot for the lead he had left himself. When he found it, he began his night's work.

The rough rope, warm from the day's sun, threaded in and out of his hands. He used his arms and elbows to hold parts of it in place as he fed rope through various loops. The rope cooled as the night air came in on a breeze. Ferrun found himself barely sweating, and he became hopeful that he might be able to get the entire rope into an organized state before the end of eternity.

The dark of night began to come to an end as the sun returned to the sky. Ferrun was able to see what he was doing, and as the full sun rose, he had a clear view of the size of the knot. Looking at the whole knot, he took in its enormity. He dropped the rope that was in his hand, letting it hang off the knot ball in such a way that he could easily find it again.

Ferrun walked away from the knot and bathed in the oasis. There hadn't been dripping in the night, and he wasn't surprised because the pool would have overflowed with water if it had kept filling. It was still early morning when he was clean and rehydrated.

Ferrun drank in the progress he'd made during the night and began to pick up the rope that lay around the knot in a scattered mess. He cleaned it up by organizing it into the neat rope balls he'd had before. By the time he retreated to the shade of his tree, he had added a full rope ball to his collection.

Ferrun got used to the pattern of working through the night and sleeping through the hot day. Some days he made significant progress, having nearly two balls collected instead of just one. Occasionally he would walk away in the morning with no new rope balls. Each day, he'd leave the knot with long strands of rope hanging from it, ready for him to pick up the next evening. Every few days, the dripping of the oasis would return.

The first time, Ferrun thought the pool was filling up even more. He wondered what that would mean for him. However, when he went to bathe the next morning, he found that the water level had receded. After a few days, the pit was empty again.

Ferrun worried that he'd get dehydrated with the water gone. But to stay alive, he merely slept longer hours in the shade, conserving his energy for the chilly nights. Those nights were less productive because the moon was full; he often found his eyes created more messes than his hands did. It took a lot of effort for him to sit still and avoid working on the project in front of him in the light of the moon.

After a few days of the pit being empty, the dripping returned and the moon's face receded. The pit filled back up with water, and Ferrun was at a point where the knot was shorter than him, although still quite wide.

Realizing that the oasis had a tide like the ocean, Ferrun cursed his luck. If he'd walked at a slower pace like Gray had wanted, the pool might have been full by the time they arrived there. He might have been able to convince Gray to turn back and find his rock. Or at least Gray wouldn't have exacted revenge on him by knotting up his rope.

***

After four cycles of the water's rising and falling, Ferrun had all of his rope free and organized into balls. Untying the knot had been a massive undertaking, but as he finished the project, he realized it hadn't been any more significant than building a boat or hiking indefinitely through a forest.

He observed his progress in the morning sun and looked at the empty and sandy desert before him. He wasn't eager to set off into a day that would get hotter as it went by. And he remembered the fresh and comfortable night air. The pool was full at this point, and he thought over how he might move forward as he bathed. Ferrun knew he could travel in the afternoon and spend the morning in a rope shelter without dying. He'd lived that way with Gray on the way to the oasis. However, he didn't like having only half a day of travel. Despite having eternity to get across the desert, he didn't want to spend any more time in the maddening place than he had to.

The alternative was to keep his day/night cycle switched and travel in the cool night air. The downside was that it'd be impossible for him to see where he was going when the moon wasn't full.

Tired from the long night's work, he napped under the oasis tree. When he awoke, he followed his rope back to where the knot used to be. When his sleepy mind remembered that he'd already unknotted everything, he realized how he could travel in the comfort of the night.

He picked up the rope that ran off away from the oasis and began to pass it hand over hand. He blindly knotted it into an organized rope ball as he collected slack, a familiar pattern he didn't think he'd ever forget how to do. The sand was smooth, and there was nothing to trip over after he got away from the tufts of oasis grass.

***

After a few nights of travel and spending the daytime sleeping in the shade of his rope hut, Ferrun fell on his face into the sand. He'd tripped on something in the dark moonless night. As he felt to see what it was, he realized it was a dead man with chapped lips and hot skin despite the cold night air.

Despite not being able to see the face, Ferrun knew who it was. Gray's rope had never been far from Ferrun's line, and he figured the man had merely followed it away from the oasis.

Gray lay dead in the desert, passed out from the heat of the sun. Over the entire month of Ferrun unknotting the rope, Gray had made the progress of only a few full days' travel. Ferrun felt bad for him because he knew the man was facing the torture of the dark void right now. He felt a strange gratefulness towards Gray and the mess he'd made with the rope. Without it, he wouldn't have learned how to travel efficiently through the desert.

Climbing back up to his feet, he found his rope again. Ferrun started making his way towards his rock again, collecting slack. Gray would notice in the morning that the rope he was traveling near was gone and that Ferrun was free from the oasis. It wouldn't make him happy. But he'd have to catch Ferrun to do anything about it, and Ferrun suspected Gray wouldn't be able to catch up to him. Gods willing, Ferrun wouldn't have to come back through this desert, and if he never met Gray again, he'd be happy.

Ferrun continued traveling night after night by the feel of his rope. He'd spent weeks traveling and had amassed a few extra balls of rope, but still there was no sign of the desert's end. However, as the sun came up above the horizon one night, Ferrun saw strange black specks in the distance. He continued towards them out of curiosity instead of making a camp at first light like he traditionally did. Curious about the specks, he wondered if they were other people.

He was shocked to discover that the specks were a field of rocks. Some moved, while others stayed still. They were all different shapes and sizes, but most of them were smaller than Ferrun's waist. The one thing all the rocks had in common was that they each had a rope attached to them. Each line led to the horizon, but they all went in the same direction as Ferrun's rope.

IV

Hills

Chapter Twenty-One

I n the shade of half a dozen trees, Ferrun slept through the after-noon. He'd made it out of the desert a few weeks after discovering what he'd come to call a herd of rocks. It was his second week of trav-eling through the forest, and he enjoyed not being under the constant barrage of the harsh sun. The trees, which were sparse at first, were now thick enough to make it difficult for him to travel blindly at night.

His body, so used to sleeping during the day and traveling at night, was still stuck in its old pattern. Afternoon naps were now more of a habit than a necessity, but it was a habit he enjoyed and had no plan to break any sooner than he had to.

Ferrun woke up lazily, estimating he still had a few hours of travel left in the day. He was in no hurry to get up. He heard someone walking past him, grunting at the rope they were dragging behind them, and he opened his eyes, full of energy. This was the first person he'd encountered since leaving the solitude of the desert. He consid-ered steering clear since his interaction with Gray had gone so poorly, though he'd met dozens of people with Teekola, and they had been little more than rude. Having survived the worst Gray could do, he reasoned that he could survive anything this new stranger could throw at him.

Following the sound of the grunting, he eventually found a woman with gray hair and a young, energetic face fighting with her rope.

"Hey, how's it going?" Ferrun called out.

She jumped at the sound of his voice. Perhaps she was as used to solitude as Ferrun was. She immediately turned to him and gave him a scowl. "Obviously not great since I'm here," she said, lifting the rope in her hand.

"That's fair," Ferrun replied genuinely. He pulled his rope balls behind him as he approached her. Once he got to a conversational distance, he sat on the ball he'd been working on.

The gray-haired woman gawked at him. "What in the world are those?" Her tone was filled with disgust rather than the typical reverence, jealousy, or amazement Ferrun's slack typically received.

"It's my rope," Ferrun said casually. He tugged on the rope, and a few of the dozens of balls he traveled with came into the clearing. "I've been collecting it."

"I see that." Wonder, or at least curiosity, was seeping into her voice. "I can't imagine why."

"Well, when they asked me what size I wanted my boulder to be, I asked for the biggest one. That seems to have been a mistake because now I can't drag it behind me." He gave a half-hearted tug on his rope to illustrate his problem.

The woman laughed at him. It was a cheery laugh, and it seemed that his situation had brought twisted joy to her day.

"What?"

"It's just funny that I spent all morning for the past few days cursing myself, this rope, and the godforsaken rock at the end of it—and then I meet you, who can't even drag the rock behind him. I'd feel bad for laughing at you, except you did it to yourself, so I..." She shrugged as though she didn't need to continue explaining, and she went back to laughing at him.

"Thanks," Ferrun said with a smile, trying to be both a good sport and the butt of the joke. "It's not all bad though. I've learned that it's a lot easier to move around with slack. Have you ever considered turning around to find your rock? It might make it easier to move than just dragging it behind you." He thought of the herd of rocks he'd seen. Many of those people were likely traveling through these woods right now.

"No, I've never considered it," the woman said thoughtfully. "I haven't had any problems moving, at least not any more than you'd expect with a fifty-kilo rock tied to your ankle."

"I've found it liberating," Ferrun said, "and those I know who have gotten to their rock have been rewarded with a lot of freedom."

The woman with the gray hair shrugged. "Thanks for the tip, buddy, but I'm pretty dedicated to making progress towards the mountain. I'll do it through sheer hard work and elbow grease."

She bent over to pick up the rope attached to her ankle and began heading out of the clearing. It happened to be in the direction of Ferrun's rope. He quickly gathered his trail of rope balls and began to follow her.

"How do you even know this is the right way to travel?" he asked once he had caught up to her. He was looping the new slack he pulled in without even thinking about it.

The woman grunted as she pulled her rock behind her. "Because it's the opposite direction of my rock."

Ferrun turned the logic over in his mind. "I started at the base of the mountain. I saw it, but I couldn't hike to it because I had no way to move my rock. So I had to turn around." He hoped that sharing more of his story would convince her to turn back.

"Sucks for you," she said, putting a loose strand of gray hair behind her ear as she continued to heave her rock behind her with its leash.

"Well, what I'm getting at is that you can't be moving in the right direction because the mountain is that way." He pointed in the direction from which she'd come.

The woman merely shrugged and continued to labor on her current course.

"And even if it's not, and both of us are wrong, you'd at least have the freedom to move and explore to find it without having to drag that heavy weight around behind you."

She gave him a disheartening glare. "That's not how mass works." She tugged at her rock, gaining another foot, then she stopped and looked at him. "Look, pal, if you want to pick up your rope and find your beloved rock, go ahead and do it." She gestured at his rope trail leading in the direction she was headed. "But I don't know why you feel obligated to preach to me about why I should do the same. Just pick up your rope and get out of here. And maybe when you find your rock and engineer some way to move it, then you can pass me on the way back to the mountain and laugh at me. But for now, I'm set on getting there the way God intended, by dragging this damn thing behind me and getting to the top of the mountain with hard work and determination."

Ferrun opened his mouth to add a retort but couldn't think of anything worth saying. The woman stared at him intently, her eyes daring him to give her another reason to go off on him. He declined to give her one. He began picking up his slack and walked away from her, and towards his rock, at a pace he knew she couldn't keep up with even if she wanted to.

***

The trees grew thicker with every day of travel. At first, he walked through patches of trees between sparse areas of grass, then he found some dense tree areas with grassy plains between. But now, a few days after arguing with the gray-haired woman, he was in the full shade of trees nearly constantly. They weren't as thick as they were at the base of the mountain, but he could tell these woods were growing thicker.

As he traveled in the morning, he heard a sound in the distance. He followed the rustling sound of leaves to find a freckle-faced man tugging at his rope almost rhythmically. Despite all the noise he was making, he still heard Ferrun's approach.

"Hey, mate, can you help me with this?" the man asked.

Ferrun shrugged and stood behind him, helping the man tug at his rope. He quickly fell into the pattern the man followed, and the two of them pulled against his stuck rock.

After thirty minutes of tugging, the stone still refused to budge, but the man was relentless. Ferrun was tired but continued to help, unsure of how to politely get himself out of the situation. Then the boulder came loose, and they toppled back, with the man landing on Ferrun.

"Hell yeah!" the man exclaimed as he scrambled to his feet. He reached out a hand to help Ferrun up. "Thanks for the help, mate. I'm Harrower."

"Nice to meet you. I'm Ferrun," he said as he massaged his tired arms. The man across from him had light red hair to match his freckles, and his arms were the size of Ferrun's thighs. He had a hard time imagining that he contributed much to this man's efforts.

"What on Kapleen is that?" Harrower said as he stared over Ferrun's shoulder.

"What's what?" The man's excitement made Ferrun spin around, expecting to see a wild animal. He had never seen one in this world, but he didn't want to be caught flat-footed by whatever shocked the bulky man.

"That rope, mate. Where the hell did you get so much? Is it all yours?" The man walked up to it, dragging his own rope behind him loosely. Once he got to Ferrun's slack, he inspected it with wide-eyed wonder. "What possessed you to collect so much?"

Ferrun pulled up a rope ball and sat on it, offering another one to the freckled man. Then he told the story of how he started at the base of the mountain and had to begin collecting rope. Harrower was fascinated and asked dozens of questions about the logistics of it all. They spent the better part of the morning on the recounting of Ferrun's journey from the mountain to where he was today.

"You know, the more you talk about this, the more it sounds like a good idea."

"Really?" Ferrun asked. A long time had passed since someone last took his suggestion. He was beginning to doubt his process as a whole.

"Yeah, every night I go to bed because I'm stuck on something or another. I can't make progress, so I go to sleep. Then I spend the morning trying to get free. If I could carry my rock, I'd make way more progress."

"That's the thought." Though Ferrun knew that even if he got to his boulder, it'd be unlikely he'd be able to lift it.

They spent the early afternoon tracing back Harrower's rope, and Ferrun showed him how to coil it in a way that rolled easily but didn't come undone.

When most of the afternoon had passed, Harrower leaned against a tree for a break. "I really appreciate you giving up some of your time to teach me. I know you've had to let out some of that slack you've collected to do it."

Ferrun shrugged at the comment, but Harrower was right; he had let out a bit, but he was going to go back and collect it. He told himself it was a small price to pay for teaching something that could change this man's afterlife.

"I'm glad you told me about this," Harrower continued. "I don't know how long it would have been until I got stuck for good, but I'm glad I met you. I'm glad you shared this idea with me. I'll make sure to tell everyone I meet. I hope you do the same. Although that already seems to be your plan."

"I'm glad you were receptive to it. A lot of people aren't."

"Well, don't let them discourage you," the burly redhead said with a smile. "They'd spoil it for the rest of us who want to hear it." He wrapped his muscular arms around Ferrun and squeezed.

Ferrun hugged the man back but thought he was soon going to pass out from the constriction. When the man let go, Ferrun sucked in a gasp of air.

"Thanks for everything, Harrower," he said.

"No, thank you. Now go on! Get back to it!" Harrower gestured in the direction where Ferrun had come.

As Ferrun collected his rope and the day wound to a close, he heard another noise in the distance. He hadn't made it back to where he'd first met Harrower, but he had a rope trail to follow.

Ferrun knew it'd be impossible for him to get lost in the woods, so he set off to find the source of the noise with Harrower's words in the back of his mind. He wondered if the person making the ruckus would also be accepting of his idea to collect rope or if they'd denounce him as crazy. Either way, he would continue to share his story and not let anyone spoil it for those who needed to hear it.

Chapter Twenty-Two

F errun gathered his rope, which no longer followed a straight path but looped in and out around the trees. He was collecting his rope mindlessly, reminiscing about his successful conversation with Jason, the guy he'd most recently met. After meeting Harrower, Ferrun continued to travel all over the forest. He'd just explained to Jason the idea of going back to find his rock. Jason liked the idea and was the fourth person open to it. The words of the burly redhead had encouraged Ferrun to keep spreading the idea.

He listened for the sound of another person as he collected his rope. They might be receptive or they might not be. He was only interested in getting his idea to more people. As he rolled his balls of rope around a tree to unknot a bit that he'd wrapped there from one of his journeys, he heard a loud curse in the distance. He dropped what he was doing and left his rope still partly knotted around the tree. He had slack, and he could always come back to unknot this loop later.

Ferrun headed in the direction of the sound. He heard the rustling of leaves once he got closer. It was the distinctive sound of someone trying to get a good grip on the ground so they could pull their rock free. Ferrun could tell the racket was close but didn't notice the person making the sound until he walked past a tall, thick tree.

On the other side of the tree was the gray-haired woman he'd met when he first entered these woods. Her youthful face was grimacing as she tugged at the rope. She was muttering curses, some of which were under her breath, while many others weren't.

"Hey, how's it going?" Ferrun asked.

The woman jumped at least a foot, dropping the rope she was pulling. "Son of a bitch! You scared me!"

Ferrun put his hands up in a gesture of surrender and backed away, saying, "Sorry! Didn't mean to."

She nodded, then looked at him with an investigative scrunch in her face. "You look familiar. Do I know you from somewhere?"

"I'm Ferrun. We met once before." He gestured at his balls of rope, thinking that while he had an ordinary face, he was, for now, the only person in these woods with this much slack.

"Oh, yeah, you're the lunatic going back to his rock. I'm Hazel. How's that whole"—she gestured at his rope to find the word—"project going for you?"

Ferrun shrugged, thinking about how little progress he'd made recently, but he was reassured by the people he'd met and helped since seeing her the first time. "It's going. Haven't made much progress towards my rock, but I'm helping out a lot of people."

"Helping them by giving them the *easy way* out."

"By sharing some logic with them, yes." Ferrun didn't appreciate this reunion. "What about you? Are you getting stuck often?"

Hazel blushed, then barked, "No, this is the first time it's happened in a few days." She picked the rope back up. "I'll get it unstuck in a minute."

Ferrun reached out to help. "Do you want a hand?" For a moment, the look on the gray-haired woman's face was discouraging, and he thought she'd say no.

"I don't see why not." Her rope was on the ground from when he'd startled her. She did an elaborate kick, bringing her foot to her waist and grabbing the rope with her hands. She then handed some of the slack to Ferrun.

The two travelers tugged at the rope, and in a few moments, they could feel that it was free.

"Thanks," Hazel said. "I could have gotten it done myself. But I appreciate the help."

"No problem. I assume I'm not going to be convincing you to turn back for your rock today."

Hazel laughed, pulling the rope over her shoulder so she could move along. "Not today, Ferrun."

Ferrun shrugged, and they parted company. He wondered how long it would be until she got stuck for a whole afternoon or a full day. Would she decide it was a good idea to turn back when she got indefinitely stuck like Gesa had? It was unbelievable he'd met her twice. He doubted he'd ever see her again or know what she'd settle on. The only solace he had was that at least she would know that the option was there. He wondered how many others were stuck in these woods or in this world and didn't even know that turning back was a viable option.

As he backtracked and picked up the slack he'd scattered across the woods, he thought it was funny that it was viable for everyone but him, even though he was the one who'd come up with it. He'd done it out of necessity. However, if he succeeded, he'd merely be stuck next to a massive boulder and unable to move towards the mountain he was supposed to climb.

Sure, Gesa had gotten to her rock, and when he talked to others, he used this as a proof of concept. But even that had ended in Gesa losing motivation for travel. When he was forced to leave her and move on towards his rock, she'd planned to explore instead of make progress.

***

For days Ferrun toiled over this conundrum as he backtracked his rope. Occasionally he'd go on short excursions, letting out slack to hunt down a sound he thought was another human. Unfortunately, he didn't find anyone and chalked the sounds up to wind or falling branches.

As he was chasing down one of these sounds and about to turn back, assuming it was nothing, he heard a whistle. It wasn't the wind whipping through tree branches but a birdlike tune. Ferrun honed in on the direction, and as he started to close in on it, he noticed the sound was coming closer.

Ferrun was so intent on paying attention to the sound that he missed noticing the rope that lifted off the ground. He tripped over it and fell into a pile of dirt and leaves. The whistling was now right next to him, but then it stopped.

"Sorry about that," the man standing above him said. He reached his hand out and helped Ferrun up.

As Ferrun dusted himself off, he noticed that the whistling man was holding a rope in one hand and a ball of rope in the other.

"No problem. Thanks," Ferrun blurted out as he racked his brain to figure out when he'd met this man and explained his idea to him. "Have we met before?" He studied the man's long hair and thin lips.

"I don't think so. I'm Jabril."

The name didn't sound familiar to Ferrun. "We have to have met. I'm Ferrun."

"You're *Ferrun*?" Jabril said in amazement.

Ferrun still couldn't remember when he'd met this man, but the man had obviously met him. "Yeah, are you sure we haven't met?"

"Oh, no, I would have remembered meeting you!" The young man sounded like a child meeting a superhero. "Harrower told me about you. He was telling me about the idea you had, and he suggested I do the same, and I have been." He lifted the small ball of rope in his hand and then gestured at another small one behind him. "It's so much easier than dragging my rock around."

Ferrun was stunned and sat down on the ground. "Harrower told you about me?"

"Yeah, and when I first heard you coming, I was excited that I'd get to tell someone else to pass the idea along and all. But then I noticed you already have rope balls, and quite a lot. I was bummed, but now I'm meeting *the* Ferrun. Do you really have thirty rope balls like Harrower said?"

Ferrun gestured over his shoulder, and the man counted.

"Twenty-nine," Jabril said after a moment. "That's pretty close to thirty."

Ferrun had a nagging thought that he should have had more than thirty but dropped it as the young man brought up questions about Ferrun's journey to this point.

"Did you really make a boat out of just rope?"

The pair sat on their balls of rope to talk. Ferrun answered the man's countless questions. They quickly learned that Harrower had shared everything with Jabril, even if he'd taken some liberty with the details.

In the end, Jabril said, "Wow, I didn't think I'd ever meet you. Harrower said you'd left to go the other direction, and I figured you'd be long gone towards your rock now."

"Me too," Ferrun said, mulling over something that was nagging the back of his mind. He looked at the long-haired man's rope ball. "How long did it take you to get that?"

"About a month. Should it be quicker?"

"No, that's about right. Do you know how many balls Harrower had when you met him?"

"Just the one," Jabril said, then eagerly added, "But I'm sure he's got more now."

"That's what I'm afraid of," Ferrun said, nodding.

Jabril made a puzzled face as Ferrun got up from his seat. Ferrun counted the rope balls and realized Jabril had counted right. There were only twenty-nine. By his last count, Ferrun had more than thirty balls. He'd backtracked his rope to make up the lost distance. However, he'd let out at least a ball of slack a month. A grim frown settled on his face.

"What's wrong?" Jabril asked.

"Nothing." Ferrun didn't want to burden the eager man with this new problem.

"Anything I can help with?"

Ferrun turned the question over in his mind along with a dozen other things he was thinking about. "Yeah, how eager was Harrower to tell you about this whole idea?"

"He brought it up before he introduced himself," the long-haired man said with a laugh.

Ferrun nodded his head as if Jabril had given him grave news. "It was good to meet you."

It was getting late, and Ferrun didn't feel like being around the eager young man while thinking up a solution for the hole he'd dug himself into. Not only was he two months behind on collecting slack; he had also let out two months of slack. He wasn't just stuck. He was moving backward.

Ferrun picked up slack and left the young man to do the same. He debated whether he should continue to traipse around the woods, sharing his idea with others, or if he should continue towards his rock. He knew arriving at his rock was pointless. Once there he wouldn't be able to budge it an inch. However, he also knew his effectiveness as a woodland messenger would diminish over time. Jabril's eagerness and Harrower's stories were proof of that.

He leaned against a tree and hopelessly slid to the ground. His eyes grew heavy with sleep, and he wondered what the right solution to his problem would be.

***

"He can't just quit his job and go to school like you do," she said, rocking the baby in her arms.

"I've got a lot going on right now. It's the end of the quarter," his father, Vito, added.

Ferrun was eating a bowl of his father's penne alla vodka. It was some of the best-tasting food he'd had in a long time. Despite being blindsided by the conversation, he replied with, "It doesn't have to be tomorrow, but it should be soon." It felt like they were following a script, and he didn't think he'd like the ending.

Emilia, his sister, said, "He's always working. He's busy. Let him be."

He ignored his sister's comment. "Padre, Mom doesn't want this for you."

"She was fine with it before," Emilia added.

"She wanted the best for us—that includes you," Ferrun said. "We're grown up and moved out. It's time to take care of yourself."

"I'm not going back to school," Vito said. "I didn't need it before. I don't need it now. I'm not like you."

"I still live here. And so does little Rosa," Emilia said.

"Then go find somewhere that will put you in charge of people," Ferrun said to his father. "There are new property management companies starting all the time. They all need accountants."

"And I'll be working for people as ignorant as Rosa," Vito said, throwing his hands up into the air.

"Then help them, teach them."

"Then they take the credit." He gestured rudely at the imaginary bosses he'd never work for. "At least here everyone knows who does the good work."

"But they don't pay you for that work."

"That's between me and them."

"You have to change something. You can't keep living like this."

"Your grandfather lived in the closet of a butcher shop for two years, saving up money to bring your grandmother over."

Ferrun tried not to roll his eyes. His grandfather had also smoked a pack of cigarettes a day and couldn't be taken into public the last ten years of his life without him uttering a slur. "Nonno got through discomfort to achieve something great. A lecture hall is better than a closet. He wanted a new life for his family."

"And we have that life." Vito gestured at the massive house full of trinkets and gadgets, most of which the man had no time to enjoy because of how much he worked.

"Look what it's costing you." Ferrun gestured at the pile of bills under the empty bread basket.

"I've got it under control. I just need a little help from mia famiglia."

"You need help from me, Padre."

"And you're not going to give it to me? I changed your diapers and wiped your ass."

"I'm sure I'll have to return that in kind." Ferrun groaned. "If I do this, then you've got to look at schools. Please?"

"I'll look into something," his father said noncommittally. "I just need something to get me through the next month."

Ferrun pulled out a checkbook from his jacket pocket. This was the uncomfortable ending he knew would come. It always came. His father was a problem bigger than Ferrun's thesis. He hoped this conversation was a good step on the path to solving it.

Chapter Twenty-Three

Ferrun woke up with his back sore from sleeping against the tree. His mind was still weighed down by the options that lay in front of him. He could continue to help others and spend eternity telling them to reach their rock to climb the mountain but never reaching his own. Or he could collect the rest of his rope, an indefinite amount, and spend the rest of eternity tethered to whatever unfortunate spot the gods put it. Either way he would have to spend eternity stuck in one place or another. His odds of getting to the top of the mountain were looking like they were slim to none. Of the two options, he'd prefer to help as many people as possible.

As if the world he was stuck in were answering his question, he heard a person clomping through the forest. He got up, happy to share his idea but unsure if it was the right choice. He dragged his rope balls behind him, letting out slack and wondering what he was going to do in a few years when the slack ran out. He saw the person in the distance. It was a young girl who couldn't be past her teens. She was dragging a rope behind her. As Ferrun was about to call out to her, he tripped on something and landed on his face. He let out a cry in pain.

"Oh my gosh!" the girl shouted from a few yards away. "Are you okay? I'll be right there."

Ferrun's nose had done him the favor of breaking his fall and had broken in the process. He held it and felt warm blood coming out. He shouted back at the girl, "I'm fine," and it came out nasally. His nose dripped blood around him, and he couldn't breathe through it. He stood up, and as he tried to move forward again, he noticed his foot attached to his rope wouldn't move. He tried to see what he had tripped over, but it wasn't easy. Eventually, between looking up to stop himself from bleeding everywhere and examining the rope, he realized his rope was caught on something.

He looked at where his rope balls were, and there was nothing wrong with them. Whatever his rope was caught on must have been farther back. He figured it could have been the tree he slept next to last night. He looked over to the girl. His nose had clotted by then. He prodded it, and it felt crooked and tender. The young woman was pulling at her rope and seemed to be stuck. Ferrun saw this and thought he could relate, but then she broke free and was able to make more progress. When she was four yards away or so, she got stuck again. She pulled again, but it was no use.

"I guess this will have to be good enough," she said, plopping down on the ground with childlike energy.

"Sorry. I'm usually more helpful than this," Ferrun said. As he spoke, he heard that he sounded muffled from his nose being clogged.

"It's fine," the girl said with a shrug. They weren't quite shouting distance, but they had to speak up to be heard. "Have you been traveling for a long time?"

"Yeah, it's been a while. Looks like it's going to be a while more." Ferrun wondered what eternity would be like stuck in one place.

The young woman wanted details about his life so far in this world, and he happily shared them as the pain in his nose faded. When he was near the end, she asked, "So, if you have all this slack, how did you get stuck?"

Ferrun shrugged. He had some ideas, but all he said was, "I'm not sure. I think someone up there just has a sense of humor." He gestured at the sky, and the whole statement reminded him of Gesa before she'd dived into the ocean to get her rock. "I think I'm going to turn back and clear up whatever mess I've made."

"Are you going to keep wandering around the forest?"

"Probably. It's the only thing worth doing."

"That's not true. You seemed so passionate about finding your rock. You've been doing this for years, and I just started. Maybe when you get to your rock it will just be a tiny little thing that's stuck in a hard-to-reach place."

"Maybe," Ferrun said, wondering if she could be right. The gods didn't owe him anything and could make up the rules as they pleased.

"You really should find your rock. I'm going to."

"Good," Ferrun said, but he could tell his heart wasn't in it.

"I really hope you don't get stuck for long. After all, if you at least make it to your rock, you'll be free to move anywhere in the world with all that slack."

He nodded absentmindedly. She was right. Gesa did gain some freedom as soon as she got to her rock. It was likely he would gain the same, even if he couldn't move it around. "Thanks."

As she wandered back to where she had come, collecting her rope, Ferrun began to do the same. For the rest of the day his broken nose was a tender reminder that he should keep his slack neat and focus on his goal instead of getting distracted by every sound in the forest. He was going to be stuck in this world, but that didn't mean he'd have to be stuck in this forest.

***

After two months of traveling and untangling his rope from the trees it had become knotted around, Ferrun found himself at the spot where he'd ditched his path for Harrower. In the grand scheme of things, he didn't know if he was any closer to his rock than when he was stuck and talking to the young girl. But he was glad to be at a point where he could move forward without worrying about his rope.

As he stood under the trees and inspected the state of his process, he heard a person moving around in the forest. Ferrun hadn't met or talked to anyone in months. He'd heard plenty of people moving through the trees, but he would only follow his rope, refusing to let out any slack regardless of how close the sound was. It was difficult, and each time he hoped his rope would take him towards the person, but fate did not comply with his wishes.

With this new sound, Ferrun considered turning to go see who it was and maybe even talk about the idea of turning back for their rock. The urge to move towards the noise gnawed at him, but he knew it was a slippery slope to being knotted in the forest again. He refused to let himself give ground despite the urge to meet another person. To compromise with his self-imposed limits, he instead sat down and waited.

He wouldn't let himself lose ground, but that didn't mean he had to walk away from the sound. It was coming from the opposite direction of his rope, and he knew if he walked away now, he would leave them behind forever. But maybe if he waited, they would stumble upon him.

Ferrun waited through the morning, and the sound slowly came closer. By afternoon, the sound hadn't made much progress, and he thought he'd be stuck there a while if he waited for them. He fought the urge to let out slack.

Finally, with a sigh of relief, he heard the sound moving again. It was growing louder, and he was confident they'd pass near him. He just wondered if they'd be close enough for him to see them, or for them to see him.

It was almost dusk when the person finally came through the trees. Ferrun had lost hope and begun debating if he should wait another day for this person or if that would be in vain. He didn't want another form of being stuck. When the person came into view, Ferrun now had no doubt their paths were fated to cross. He figured her shocked expression was mirrored on his face.

From behind a tree, the gray-haired woman Hazel appeared. She noticed him on the ground, as his dirty but white linens stood out from their brown and green surroundings. She jumped, startled by him. He put his hands up to show he was harmless.

"Of all the godforsaken people I could have run into," Hazel said, exasperated.

"You're not very high on my list either, thank you very much." Ferrun was glad to see another person, but Hazel was a lost cause if he'd ever met one.

"How are you not kilometers away from me by now? I've been traveling for two months. Have I been going in circles?"

He was uncomfortable with the accuracy of her statement. "It's a long story," Ferrun started, then added, "Well, not that long in the grand scheme of things."

Hazel looked at the sky, which was dimming from the sunset. "I'm not likely to make it much further today. And I haven't talked to anyone since the last time we ran into each other."

Ferrun could only imagine how lonely she might be. "I'll make a fire and we can talk."

The stick-rubbing method came back to him quickly, and memories of the bonfire on the beach and his time with Gesa returned. He hoped that she was doing well, and he wondered how her progress was coming on the map of the world she wanted to make. He thought one would surely come in handy if he decided to wander and share his idea after he had found his rock.

At dusk, after Ferrun had gathered enough wood for a nice long fire, he dove into the story about how he'd knotted himself all around the forest. He listened to Hazel talk about how she had gotten lost, not knowing which direction the mountain was. She lamented about how the forest had no landmarks, and Ferrun said it wasn't as bad as the desert, which got a cheerful laugh out of her.

The entire night they avoided the conversation of turning back for their rock. Ferrun didn't know if she was glad about this, but he was glad he didn't feel the burden of failure after having talked to her about it. When the fire died after a few hours, the two of them lay down against separate trees and slept through the night.

In the morning, Ferrun said, "Last night you were complaining about not having a clear direction."

Hazel looked at him, and in the light of the morning sun, he could see how eager she was to roll her eyes, "I swear! If you tell me to turn back for my rope—"

Ferrun cut her off before she could finish her threat. "No, no, no... I was going to suggest we travel together, following my rope. I could help you get your rock unstuck, and you'd at least be moving in a clear direction rather than in circles."

Hazel looked at him, mulling the suggestion over. "Does your rope lead towards the mountain?"

Ferrun shrugged. "I doubt it. But I also doubt it goes in a full circle, meaning you'd be making some kind of progress."

Hazel scratched her head, messing her gray hair up a little. "You wouldn't move as fast."

"I have the better part of eternity to follow this rope. Speed went out the window a while ago."

"I'll try it out, but if I see any promise or hope that the mountain is in another direction, I'm abandoning you and your crackpot rope-chasing idea."

"That's more than fair," Ferrun said. Thinking of how far he'd traveled since he'd gotten to this world, he was doubtful that she or anyone else he'd met in the forest would be seeing the mountain anytime soon. According to the count of his rope balls, it was at least a three-year journey and across the ocean.

"And the last thing is you can't bring up turning back for my rock," Hazel added.

"Not a problem," Ferrun agreed. He was done going out of his way to share the idea with others. It had only gotten him knotted up in more ways than one.

***

Ferrun helped Hazel tug at her rope. It was the third day in a row now, and Ferrun knew they were about to begin their regular argument that had first happened after a good hour of tugging it. Hazel dropped the rope from her hands and let out an exasperated sigh.

Ferrun followed suit and dropped the rope but held off on the sigh. She sat on one of his balls of rope leaning against a tree. She'd gotten quite used to taking the liberty of using his rope for comfort during the time they'd spent traveling together.

"You going to go on today?" she asked him. It was the beginning of the argument she was eager to have every time she was stuck.

Ferrun looked at the trail of his rope that led away from the area. "No, not today."

"You really should. I've been holding you back more and more lately." Her tone was encouraging, but Ferrun didn't have the heart to leave her wandering in circles again.

"I'm not going to leave you. Honestly, you're doing more good for me than I thought you would."

"Likely story." She blew air over her lips to prove how much she doubted his claim.

"No, really. Your rock will come free, and then we'll be making progress again. It's a good rhythm."

"Yeah, but what if it doesn't come free this time?"

Ferrun was used to this question; it would always come at this point in the argument. "It'll come free. It always comes free."

She rolled her eyes. "Just because it always comes free doesn't mean it *will* always come free."

Ferrun had taken enough statistics classes to know she was right. "It definitely won't come free if we just sit here and plav about it." *Plav* was a word he'd learned from her, and he had just learned how to use it properly. It was her word for chatting.

She rolled her eyes and he smiled at her. "Fine." She drew the word out to show that, while she might be agreeing to continue, she wasn't thrilled about it. Then she kicked her ankle up to her hand and was able to grab her rope from there. She handed some of the slack to Ferrun and they pulled again.

Ferrun fell on top of her as soon as they gave it their first coordinated pull. He had Hazel to break his fall, but she hadn't been so lucky. He rolled off her and turned to see her sitting up in the dirt of the forest floor, rubbing her head and cursing.

"Sorry about that," Ferrun said.

"Don't be," she said in a tone that didn't convince him she'd truly forgiven him. "The rock's free." She smiled, lifting up her rope.

The pair stood up and dusted themselves off. Soon they were hiking up a gradual incline while Ferrun collected his rope and Hazel pulled her rope behind her.

Chapter Twenty-Four

"Think this is the mountain?" Hazel asked as they took a break, huffing from the work of climbing the small hill.

Ferrun laughed. He was the only one of the two who had actually seen the mountain. "No, it wouldn't have snuck up on us like this. You can see that thing from a distance."

"Well, let's get to the top of this hill at the least," she said with a sigh. She did the kicking motion with her foot, and Ferrun wondered how many times she'd had to do that to get good at it.

He began collecting rope and heading towards the top of the hill when he noticed that Hazel wasn't behind him. He could tell because he heard her cursing, a usual sound, but it sounded too far away. He turned to find that she hadn't made any progress from where they had stopped to rest. He walked back down the hill to meet her.

"The damn thing is stuck again!" she shouted at him.

"It's fine," he said calmly.

"We just got it unstuck," she complained. "We haven't moved a kilometer."

"It's fine."

Hazel started tugging on the rope maniacally.

"Hey, hey, hey." Ferrun tried to calm her down. "Everything's fine. Don't worry about it. You're wasting a lot of energy just yanking on it like that."

Hazel threw her rope down on the ground, and it kicked up dust as she did. She moved towards a tree in the direction from which they'd come; it was the only way she could go. She slumped against the tree, and Ferrun thought she was going to start bawling.

He considered asking what was wrong, but the evidence was obvious. He settled on saying, "Everything's going to be all right."

She rolled her eyes as if that was all she needed to do to prove he was wrong.

"We'll get unstuck. We always get unstuck. Don't worry."

"What happens when I don't get unstuck?" She spoke the words quietly as if she were concerned someone would overhear them and make them true. "Or, even worse, what if I stay stuck for so long that you decide to go on without me? You never get stuck."

"I don't get stuck, but I'm also not making progress towards anything aside from my rock. You're at least trying to move towards the mountain."

"There's no point," she said with growing frustration. "One of these days I'm going to get so stuck that you'll have no choice but to leave me. Maybe I'll be stuck a week, or a month, or a year. Eventually you'll get fed up with being stuck in one place."

"You're not going to get stuck that long."

"You don't know that!"

"I've met a lot of people. The only people who stay stuck are the ones who want to stay stuck. Do you want to be stuck forever?"

She glared at him. They both knew the answer.

"Then let's get the rock unstuck." Ferrun bent over to pick up her rope.

"It's just going to get stuck again," Hazel said with all hope gone from her voice.

"Then we'll unstick it when that happens as well. The first person I met here was a woman who was at the base of the mountain and kept moving despite being stuck for long periods. She just kept tugging at the rope and became free eventually. She was at the base of the mountain, yet she still found a way to be unstuck."

"Yeah, and according to you, I'm three years away. And I'm already getting stuck. That's not a positive indicator."

"I know you'll make it to the top of this hill and then the top of the next one, and eventually you'll make it to the mountain." Ferrun's positivity reminded him of Teekola, who'd often encourage him like this. He knew he wasn't doing as good a job as the Captain though.

"Fine." She spit the word out as though it were less work to agree and get unstuck than to continue to argue with him.

***

"I think we'll make it to the peak of this thing before nightfall," Ferrun said.

Then he heard Hazel trip and curse. It had taken them a week to get unstuck from the first spot on the hill. Then they were stuck three more times in a week and a half. Today they'd spent nearly half the day traveling up the hill.

Ferrun turned around. He was worried even though he knew what was happening. "Are you okay?"

She glared at him as if his question was an insult. "It's fine!" She then softened her voice. "Just stuck...again." Her knee had a scrape on it, and Ferrun saw some blood when she rolled up her pant leg to examine it.

"Ouch," he said.

"I'll live." She looked up at him with a dark smile.

Ferrun chuckled but didn't think her morale was up for too many more jokes. She dusted herself off after getting to her feet. To start the routine of getting her unstuck, he bent over to pick up her rope.

"Don't," Hazel said. She kicked her foot in a way that put the rope out of Ferrun's reach.

"What?" He was still bent over, and he shuffled towards the rope.

"It's not worth it. Just go up to the top of that hill and see what there is to see. Like you said, you'll make it there before night. Just come back and tell me what's up there."

"Why do you care? It's just a hill. What we see from up there will just be more trees. Like what we see looking down this side." He gestured at the view behind them.

"No, this is a hell of a hill. Something doesn't want to let me make it to the top."

Ferrun doubted that. "I'm not going to the top of that hill without you. Even if it takes us a year."

"What if it takes two years?"

"Then it takes two years, I have all of eternity stuck in this place. I'm not in any hurry to get to my rock anyway. All odds point to it being unmovable, and that's my own fault."

"You didn't know what you were getting yourself into, kind of like how you don't know what you're getting yourself into here waiting on me."

"Come on, let's move this thing." Ferrun stepped on her rope to keep her from kicking it away from him again, then picked it up.

He heard Hazel sigh, but since she was behind him, he missed out on the elaborate eye movement he knew she was making at him.

Ferrun dug his feet in and got a good grip on the rope. "Ready?"

Hazel gave an unenthusiastic confirmation.

"One, two, three!" Ferrun counted, then he heaved on the rope. Immediately he felt it move out from whatever it was stuck on.

"Holy cow!" Hazel exclaimed in amazement.

Ferrun felt her release her grip on the rope, but he wasn't done. He kept pulling on the rope, dragging the rock closer and closer to them. It wasn't light, but he could drag it alone with a little effort.

"What are you doing?" Hazel asked with confusion.

Slack started piling up in stacking loops next to Ferrun. Between breaths and heaves, he said, "I'm finding out if you're going to get stuck again before we reach the top of this hill."

Hazel gave him a cockeyed look, but he ignored it and kept pulling. The rope got stuck after he'd piled up what he assumed would be a little over a hundred yards. Hazel jumped in at that point to help him unstick it, and it was a surprisingly quick effort.

By the time night fell, Ferrun and Hazel had pulled what Ferrun thought was about four hundred yards of rope. As the sun set behind the hill, he estimated that the crest was not much more than three hundred yards away.

"That should be good enough," Ferrun said. "We'll be able to make it to the top of the hill in the morning. Nothing can stop you now."

***

That night Ferrun could barely sleep. From the rustling he heard from Hazel, he figured she was having the same problem.

"You ever wonder what we did to earn this trial?" Hazel said into the moonless night after Ferrun rolled around on his rope pallet.

"I've heard a few theories," he replied. "But I barely know what I did in life, so it's tough to fit the pieces together."

"You were from the Old World. Earth. Right?"

They'd talked about their lives a bit but nothing more than funny stories and friends.

"Yeah, a few decades after we'd gone to the moon."

"How old were you when you died?"

"According to the memories I have, I was in my early thirties."

Hazel cursed. "I knew people died young back then, but thirty? That's barbaric."

"How old were you?"

"Late three hundreds."

"You were over three hundred years old?!" Ferrun figured she'd just misspoke.

"Our anti-aging methods were effective. Except when they weren't."

"How'd you die?"

"My treatments weren't taking effect like they were supposed to. There were complications in the process."

"Is that normal?"

"It's rare but not unheard of. But compared to thirty years old, it was a long enough life. You know what I was doing at thirty?"

"Beginning your career?"

Hazel laughed. "I didn't do that until after hitting eighty. By the time I was thirty, my parents hadn't entered cryostasis yet, so I was still living off their money. Saw the galaxy, got into some trouble. Got some people I met out of trouble. It was a mess. I didn't know anything. I still don't feel I know much after three hundred years."

"How long have you been here pulling your rock?"

"Not sure. Less than a decade. I thought I was immortal in my life, but here, faced with genuine immortality, it's not something I've grasped yet."

"Why do you think we got this trial?" Ferrun asked, coming back to the original question.

"It has to be because of our actions in life. I was a good person—not perfect but as good as I could be."

"I don't think I lived long enough to be good enough for the gods."

"That is a quandary that religion has wrestled with for millennia. How can we ever be good enough compared to a god?"

"I'm not sure these gods are flawless," Ferrun lamented, thinking of the storm on the sea and the hangman's hopeless situation.

"But even if these gods aren't flawless, all-knowledgeable, or even all-powerful, they'd want to add people to their ranks who can at least make the most of their admirably immense powers."

"And you think how we live is the way they find people?"

"It wouldn't be the goodness of our actions that necessarily qualified us for this trial but the way we faced problems in life."

Ferrun thought back to how he'd dealt with his father and how he'd responded in those memories. "I don't think I was perfect at facing problems."

"I tried to do more than most with my position in life, yet it fell short by other's standards. But that's the nature of politics." Hazel let out a big yawn. "Maybe only gods with the whole picture in mind can clearly see what made us stand out."

Ferrun found her yawn contagious. He rearranged himself on his rope pallet. "Want to try to get some sleep?"

"Might as well try."

***

When the first glint of sunlight came over the horizon behind them, Ferrun cracked his eyes open, still tired from the late night. Hazel was wide awake, leaning against a tree and messing with something in her hands.

"You ready to go?" she asked.

Ferrun noticed the thing she was messing with was her rope. She'd braided it into an elegant pattern, making it thicker and shorter. "Yeah." He hated being the one in her way just for a little more sleep. "I'll be ready in a minute."

As he said it, Hazel pulled on both ends of the rope, and the braid she'd made withered away into a single strand again. "Great," she said with eyes full of determination. Ferrun wondered if she'd gotten any sleep, or if she even needed it.

They covered the steep ground in silence, and it took them only half an hour or so to reach the crest. Ferrun felt like the slow one this time as he knotted his rope into its balls while Hazel merely had to let out her slack. She went slowly for him, and he was grateful even though they were both eager to get to the top.

As they crested the hill, the sun seemed to do the same behind them. The forest in front of them was flooded with the red and purple colors of the early morning sunlight.

"I can't freakin' believe it," Hazel said as she looked at what stood in front of them.

Ferrun was stunned by what he saw. He leaned against a tree because he thought he'd fall backward down the hill if he didn't.

"Oh my God! Oh my God! Oh my God!" Hazel repeated.

Out of the corner of his eye, Ferrun could see her bouncing up and down. But he refused to drag his eyes from the behemoth before him.

"Ferrun, are you okay?" Hazel asked, grabbing his arm.

"It's really there?"

"Yeah, it's there," she answered slowly.

Ferrun let out a breath that he hadn't realized he was holding. It was the mountain—the same mountain he'd left behind to go find his rock. It was now standing in front of him, and his rope was leading him straight to it.

"It's so close, but I left it so far behind." Ferrun felt his world spinning, and he had to lean against a tree and sit down.

Hazel laughed at the statement. "Did you never consider that the world was round?"

Ferrun shook his head. The thought had genuinely never occurred to him. "I just assumed the gods had created this world as a flat plane extending to infinity on all sides."

Ferrun took his eyes off the mountain long enough to see Hazel roll her eyes at him. Then he quickly looked back as if the thing were going to disappear right in front of him.

"It's so close. We're going to make it," Ferrun finally said as he collected his thoughts.

"No, Ferrun, you'll make it. I'm turning back."

"You're what?" He was confused. He wasn't able to put the pieces together.

"I'm turning back. I'm tired of getting stuck. I know where the mountain is now. It's only going to get harder from here."

"Yeah, but we'll get you unstuck when you have a hard time."

"No, it's too much time and work and energy. It's so frustrating to constantly be stuck. I didn't sleep last night. I just played with the slack, and it felt so freeing. I can't explain it. This morning was effortless. I want the rest of my ascent towards the mountain to be that way."

Ferrun looked at Hazel. For once, her face wasn't doing something strange to undermine such an idea. "You're serious."

"As a heart attack."

Ferrun gave her a look but understood the sentiment. "I guess I'm happy for you."

"You've finally converted me to your ways."

"I'll miss the company," Ferrun said as he stood up.

"Me too, but I'll always remember you." She moved to hug him.

Ferrun embraced her, his face pressing into her gray hair. He felt a warm tear roll down his cheek, and the water was salty on his lips. He was closing in on the mountain, and he'd met and left so many memorable people in the process. Each one had changed his life and helped him get to the top of this hill to look upon the mountain once again.

***

It was late at night and Ferrun couldn't sleep. His childhood room was littered with the toys and video games he and his brother had used that day. His parents were shouting in the other room. Neither of them used an inside voice at the best of times, and this was far from the best of times.

"I didn't want to do this in the first place," Vito said.

"I know you didn't want to," Ferrun's mother replied. "But it's what's best for the kids, and you."

"And now we're in this big mess because of it. We can barely afford this house, let alone two."

"We'll figure it out."

"We shouldn't have moved in the first place."

"It's too late for that," Ferrun's mother said calmly. "Now it's time to figure out where to go from here. We have options."

Ferrun put a pillow over his head as his dad said some adult words about their options. Their conversation died down as they moved from the living room to their bedroom. He heard the snap of the door close, and the conversation became all but muted.

Chapter Twenty-Five

S weating from the exertion of hiking up the latest hill, Ferrun took a break at the top. He corralled his rope balls so they wouldn't roll back down. He was up to thirty balls now, and he worried they'd drag him back down the hill if he wasn't careful. He caught his breath as he looked across the land in front of him. The terrain was more rugged on this side of the mountain.

From the top of the hill, he could see movement through the trees. He spotted half a dozen people through the rare gaps in the trees. They were fiddling with their rope. He assumed they were working towards the mountain, but maybe the word had spread enough that some were headed back to their rock.

He looked out to find his rock, scanning for it on the horizon and between the gaps of trees. When Merc, the god who had assigned him his rock, asked what size he wanted, Ferrun had said he wanted the biggest one they had. He didn't know at the time why he decided to commit to something so extreme. He'd cursed himself for it a lot in the beginning, and he still did some days, but the more he learned of his past, the more he realized he wasn't one to shy away from a challenge. That didn't stop him from regretting the decision occasionally.

Scanning the horizon, he hoped that the biggest one they had would be visible from where he stood. The fact that he couldn't see it indicated one of two things. It was either past the mountain or shorter than some of the trees. He looked up at the tree next to him. It was so tall that he couldn't reach the lowest branches. He had considered climbing but decided against it, thinking it might take him a day or two to get to the top. If his rock was that height and had an equally large diameter, Ferrun wondered if he would even be able to move it.

Having caught his breath, he began traveling down the hill. He could hear a person traveling through the woods. They were making a racket. He considered going to find them but thought better of it. It'd be difficult to convince someone who could see the mountain to turn back. He returned to coiling his rope and daydreaming about how he might move his rock. The rock would crush most things with its weight, and surely as the trees got thicker closer to the mountain, he wouldn't be able to fit the boulder between them. Ferrun began to imagine solutions to moving his rock towards the mountain, and he worried about what was hidden among the tall trees.

He cut off the daydreams when he realized that the mountain was so steep and rugged in places that there'd be almost no way to drag the rock up without it sliding back down or getting stuck. His hope escaped with a sigh, and he tried not to think about how each step he took was taking him closer to the rock that would bind him to one place for eternity.

As Ferrun continued, he got closer to the sound of the other traveler, and he got excited about the prospect of seeing another person.

A gap in the trees let him see far up the mountain. He could see where the greenery of the forest grew on the sides and the line where it stopped. After that there was bare rock where nothing seemed to grow. It became white after a few more feet before disappearing into the clouds.

He wondered how much further it reached past the clouds, but they were always up there blocking the top from view. Each time he saw mountain, he wondered if one day the winds would change and remove the veil from the peak. He doubted this and even considered it being for his own good, since if he could see how high the mountain was, he might give up all hope there and then.

A man who looked about Ferrun's age with dark black hair and a skinny build was walking while looking down at Ferrun's rope. He was traveling with strands of loose slack, some of which was draped around his shoulders, while the rest dragged limply in the dirt behind him. If Ferrun had been coiling his rope as intently as this man was staring at it, the two would have run into each other.

"Hey there," Ferrun said, breaking the man from his trance.

The man stood up straight, and the ropes fell off his back into a tangled pile. He looked at Ferrun with pure wonder. He began to say something, stopped, then started again.

When nothing came out the second time, Ferrun introduced himself.

The man tripped over a few words, then spat out, "Liyu. I'm Liyu. This rope." He gestured to the rope on the ground with reverence. "It belongs to you?"

"Yes, it's mine rope." Ferrun pointed a thumb at the rope balls it led to. He displayed his ankle to the man as if the knot had some identification to it.

The man looked at him in disbelief. He looked at him so intently that his face wound up turning red.

"Can I help you?" Looking at the mess of rope, Ferrun knew there was at least one way he could help the man out.

"It's really you," Liyu said.

"Are you headed back to your rock? Why do you have so much rope just lying around? Surely it gets caught on things."

"Yes, it gets caught all the time. I've been following your rope for a long time now."

"Following my rope?" Ferrun said in bewilderment. "Why? Follow your own rope. Then you'll find your rock and be able to go anywhere in this world." He had assumed this man was just another person who had gotten the message of his idea. He was surprised anyone would undergo such a long journey without winding their rope tightly. He now worried his message was getting mixed up the more it was shared.

"Follow my rope?" Liyu sounded just as confused as Ferrun. "Why would I do that? Mine's just attached to a rock far away. I've been fighting with it my whole way to the mountain."

"You're not headed to the mountain though." Ferrun began pointing out the obvious since the not so obvious was confusing Liyu.

"I've been there. That's where I found your rope. So I decided to follow it back."

"My rope passes by the mountain?" Ferrun asked. It was strange that he didn't think he would pass so closely to the mountain on his journey to his rock.

"Of course it goes to the mountain," the man said. "It doesn't just pass by it though. It's attached to it."

"Attached to what?"

"Attached to the mountain," Liyu said slowly. "I assumed you knew. I assumed you told the gods to attach you to the mountain so you could climb it easier."

"My rope isn't attached to the mountain." Ferrun dismissed the idea as ridiculous.

"Yes, it is." The man dragged the words out as if saying them slower would put them more concretely into Ferrun's head.

"Like on a really big rock that's sitting on the mountain?"

"No," Liyu said with a bit of snicker. "It's attached to a little out-cropping that no one can reach. There's a bit of rope looped around it with a knot like the one on our ankles."

"I can't be attached to the mountain. I asked for the biggest boulder they had, and so they gave me something really heavy. You followed the wrong rope."

The man laughed. "Something heavy is accurate. That mountain has to be the biggest thing in this world. That is some clever phrasing. If you had outright asked to be attached to the mountain, they surely would have denied you."

"I'm really attached to the mountain?" Ferrun asked quietly as if speaking it too loudly would shatter it.

"Yes. You're attached to the mountain, and there are about a dozen people waiting near the knot to meet you. Although some of them think you'll never show up."

Ferrun would have agreed with those people until a few minutes ago. Now his world had changed. Dragging his rock was indeed an impossible task. It had been impossible from the start, but now he knew it wasn't necessary—assuming what this stranger was saying was accurate.

***

"Are you sure that you followed the right rope?" Ferrun asked. The pair had spent the day getting to know each other and collecting their rope. The sun had set behind the mountain a while ago, and that was when they decided to lie down for the night.

Liyu nodded. "I am absolutely sure. It's not like there's that many out here to follow." He was wrapping the mess of slack he had collected that day per Ferrun's instructions.

"Hold on. Don't wrap it like that." Ferrun waved his hand at the young man's mess of rope. "If you wrap it like that, you won't be able to get the rope out when you need it. It will stay tight in a ball."

"Isn't that the idea?" Liyu asked.

"No, the point is that it's easy to move when it needs to move but gives you slack when you need slack." Ferrun tied the type of knot he wanted him to do.

"That's what I did," Liyu complained.

"No, it's not." Ferrun untied the knot, moving his hands so fast that it looked like magic. "This is what you did." He tied a similar knot.

"That's the same thing."

"Nope," Ferrun said, offering the loose end to his new companion. "Pull."

Liyu pulled and nothing happened. "It doesn't do anything."

"Exactly. It will pull fine, but it won't let slack out when you need it." Ferrun untied it, then retied the ideal knot. "Pull now."

Liyu pulled lightly on the rope and again nothing happened. "It's the same knot," he complained.

"Pull harder."

Liyu did as he was told, and after he overcome the initial friction of the knot, the ball let out its slack. The man's eyes widened in amazement. "It's the same knot."

"No, it's not," Ferrun said slowly. "It's a similar knot, but the second to last overhand should be an underhand." He untied the knot to the point where the man was making the mistake. "Here's where it matters." He slowly tied the underhand loop to show Liyu the right move.

"Okay, thanks."

They'd spent the better part of the evening tying rope, and this was Liyu's last ball of rope to tie together. How he'd been traveling with loose slack over his shoulder Ferrun would understand.

Ferrun pulled the knot loose. "Now you try."

Liyu's face deflated when he realized he was going to have to tie the knot all over again himself.

"Don't worry. It's easy," Ferrun assured him. "It's going to be important for you to know how to do this right when you head back towards your rock."

"I'm not going towards my rock," Liyu protested. "I'm returning to the mountain with you."

"I'm not headed towards the mountain," Ferrun said, then added, "This is the part."

Liyu looked at the two lines of rope in his hands. He was about to do an overhand knot, but then he swapped his hands to make an underhand knot. "Thanks."

"I'm sure you saw someone's rope tied to the mountain, but it wasn't mine. I'm tied to a massive immovable boulder somewhere in this world. I didn't ask Merc to tie me to the mountain." He'd seen how this man handled rope and was sure he'd gotten Ferrun's mixed up with another rope tied to the mountain. There was no point in getting his hopes up on something so ridiculous.

Liyu stood up, excited that his last ball of rope was complete. "That's what the mountain is. Just a massive rock that doesn't move. You think there's anything bigger on this planet?"

"It's a mountain. It's made up of a bunch of rocks," Ferrun said, dismissing the man's point.

"I don't know. It looked pretty solid to me."

"Plus, the mountain was here before I showed up. They didn't just create it for me."

"What's time to gods?" Liyu asked.

Ferrun shrugged. He had no energy to argue with him.

"Don't worry. We'll be there in no time," the man claimed in excitement. "It took me a while to get here, but that's because my rock was being stubborn. Now we're both picking up slack, so it should be easier."

***

As they traveled Liyu explained that he'd gotten to the mountain and stayed there for a while. When he saw that nothing interesting was happening with the rope, he decided to investigate who was attached to the other end.

"So you were pulling your rock closer to the mountain every day as you walked towards me?"

Liyu shrugged. "I guess so. I don't really pay attention to these things."

Ferrun was not surprised by that statement.

Liyu and Ferrun came across some trees that separated them, something that happened occasionally. Liyu had to diverge from Ferrun's path, as his rope was weaved between various trees. Ferrun waited for the day it would diverge but didn't let his hopes get too high.

"So you just quit following my rope every once in a while?" Ferrun asked when they merged together again.

"I think my rock was really stuck here, and I had to pull on it a bunch. Once it got free, I realized your rope wasn't near me anymore."

"But instead of backtracking you continued on?"

"Didn't really see the point in going back to the mountain. I already knew what was there. Besides, people would make fun of me for coming back empty-handed. They said I would be doing a lot of work for nothing."

Divergences like these gave Ferrun the feeling that his rope wasn't the one tied to the mountain. Some other clever fellow had asked for it specifically and of course was probably at the top by now.

"These other people. Who are they?"

"Just people like me who made it to the mountain but thought it was too much work to ascend it."

Ferrun imagined a camp of people just sitting around his rope, waiting for something to happen instead of making progress. He felt bad for the person who would eventually get their focus.

Chapter Twenty-Six

After a few months of travel, Liyu was better at tying up rope balls. He still preferred to travel with the slack draped around his neck during the day. He claimed it was easier for him to knot it all up in the evening. Tying up rope as he walked was second nature to Ferrun, and he thought he'd feel weird walking somewhere without picking up rope.

"So after all this work, you don't think it's easier to go back to your rock than it is to pull your rock behind you?" Ferrun asked while the man knotted his rope by firelight.

"Sure, it might be, but I'm not studied at making these rope balls. I'll likely get it all knotted up on the way. I made it this far just by pulling the rock behind me."

Ferrun nodded at this, wondering how the man would have done it without Ferrun teaching him the ropes. "You know, the whole way out here, you were pulling your rock towards the mountain."

Liyu was silent about this for a while. "Huh... I guess I could probably be halfway up the mountain by now."

"It at least means you didn't have to get stuck at the base of the mountain with those people."

"I guess. But it did seem pretty stuck when I got there. When I started following it back to you, it became a little easier to pull but not much." He thought about this as he focused on the knot he was tying, "Maybe it's at a different angle."

"Maybe," Ferrun said, not convinced it was as simple as that.

"Where did you learn all of these knots?" Liyu asked. "Were you a fisherman or sailor?"

"No," Ferrun said with a laugh. "I didn't do much on the ocean until I got here."

"Who taught you all this then?"

"I figured it out, experimented. I was a researcher."

"What does a researcher do?"

"Figure out new stuff. I'm sure there were researchers in your time."

"I studied a lot, but it was to work in the government. Did you research for the government?"

"No, I avoided that kind of stuff. Didn't pay as well as commercial use. What did you study?"

"Laws, traditions, poetry, and philosophy. I took the imperial examination. I hoped to make my family proud."

"How'd you do?"

Liyu shrugged, and some of the rope slipped off his shoulders. "Not sure."

"You didn't get the results?"

"Sometimes I do well, sometimes I fail, sometimes I'm robbed on my way home from the exam."

"The dreams aren't consistent?" Ferrun knew the sensation.

"I hope I did well enough that my family could be proud of me."

"I'm sure they are."

"But now I've been given this exam, and I'll make my family proud completing it."

"I'm sure you will," Ferrun said with a smile.

***

The next day the two men came across an area where Liyu's rope was weaved between multiple trees. It was worse than the regular divergent paths Liyu typically took.

"What on Earth were you doing here?" Ferrun asked when he saw the mess that Liyu had created with his rope.

"Oh my gosh! This is it!" Liyu exclaimed. "I did this the first night because I thought it would help me get some leverage on the rope. I wanted to use the trees like pulleys. Unfortunately, it didn't work, but it means we're only a day away."

Ferrun's heart fluttered in his chest. "Only a day?"

"Yeah, I remember the first night here. It was so long ago."

The two men continued, and Ferrun could see that Liyu was bubbling with excitement. Ferrun was nervous of what he would find by the end of the day. So far, they hadn't found anyone else's rope that Liyu might have crossed paths with.

After midday the two men began to hear voices in the distance. In less than an hour they came out of the forest into a small cultivated clearing. Ferrun saw a dozen or so people sitting around in shaded areas or hanging on rudimentary hammocks. A few people looked up to gawk at the new arrivals.

"Afternoon, everyone," Liyu said, getting the group's attention. "I want to introduce everyone to Ferrun." He spread his arms wide as he presented Ferrun to the group.

Ferrun felt his face heat up in embarrassment. He followed his rope, picking up a little bit and trying to ignore all the stares. As he moved further into the clearing, his rope balls came out of the forest behind him. He heard a few gasps, but his focus was elsewhere. His rope led a few feet up the mountain. His eyes had to follow it the rest of the way since he could no longer collect it.

On a little outcropping of rock attached to the side of the mountain above him was a simple knot that had a rope hanging down from it. That rope led to the loops in Ferrun's hand, through the almost forty balls of slack he had gathered, and to his ankle.

His vision became blurry as he stared at the knot that connected him to the mountain. He rubbed his eyes to clear them, and he noticed they were wet.

Liyu was right. Ferrun's rope was attached to the mountain.

***

Ferrun stared at the knot attached to the rocky outcropping. The rope hung off it and sloped gently to his hand. When he pulled it, the line went taut.

"Ferrun. Hey, Ferrun." Liyu seemed to be calling from a distance.

Ferrun was startled by a hand on his shoulder. "Huh? What?"

"Hey, are you okay?" Liyu said, giving him a concerned look.

"Yeah, I'm fine." Ferrun pulled his eyes away from the knot that attached him to the mountain. As he turned around, he saw a crowd of people gathered around him, staring at either him or his knot. Some seemed amazed, while others murmured to each other, perhaps trying to make sense of what was going on. There was even a man who seemed so unamused with the situation that he picked his teeth with his pinky, seemingly out of boredom.

"Hi," Ferrun said, addressing the crowd. He wasn't sure what they wanted from him, or if they wanted anything at all. He wondered if they would tie him up like Gray had, jealous of his progress. There wasn't much he could do to fight back against the whole group. Trying to relax and take in the situation, he leaned against his rope ball and took a seat.

"Where did all that rope come from?" a man in the crowd asked.

Ferrun's rope balls were scattered through the clearing. Some were among the crowd, while others sat near him. "It's the slack that connects me to my rock." The words were routine for him now, but their meaning had changed.

"How did you wind up attached to the mountain?" a woman asked. She had taken the liberty of sitting on a rope ball like he had.

"I don't know," Ferrun said. "I just asked for them to attach me to the biggest rock they had."

"How did you know that would work?" someone Ferrun couldn't make out shouted from the back.

Up until a few minutes ago, Ferrun hadn't known it worked. He'd regretted taking on the challenge and wished he hadn't found himself in this afterlife. "It's a long story."

"Go on then," said the woman sitting on his rope ball. A few others took seats as well, looking at him expectantly.

He began the story he'd told a dozen times before. He talked about his travels from the base of the mountain and about building the boat with Gesa. He'd practiced the story by telling it to a few people individually. This was the largest group he'd ever addressed. They listened patiently, asking questions throughout. When night fell, someone started a campfire, and they continued to talk around it. Some of the people's questions were about the details of the story, while others were about the entire idea of turning back towards his rock.

Ferrun finally arrived at the end of the story, the part that brought him here, and he found that no one had fallen asleep out of boredom.

For the first time it felt like a story that had an ending, like he wasn't just going to leave his audience wondering if he'd succeed.

By the time he finished, most of the crowd looked half asleep. He was exhausted from the day's travel and recounting the story. A few people had more questions, but most thanked him for his story and wandered off to whatever hammocks and pallets they'd built to sleep on.

***

The young boy looked up at his mother and yawned. She was talking to his father, a lighthearted argument, one he would soon be used to.

"We can't name him Ferruccio," she complained. She held her fingers above the child's head and wiggled them. The boy reached out for them playfully, taking in the world around him with wide eyes.

"It's a saintly name, Susan. It was my grandfather's name and the name of the creator of the Lamborghini."

The boy cooed as he stared at the clean white room around them.

"It's going to be unpronounceable for all his teachers."

His father scoffed in his soon-to-be-familiar way. "That's their problem, not his."

"Ferruchio, Ferrusio, Fairutio..." His mother listed every mispronunciation she could while rocking the boy back and forth. "What about Ferrum?"

"That's not an Italian word."

"It's Latin."

"Merely a first draft." His father waved his hand to brush the language away.

"It's the word for iron," she explained in her patient way. "It's why the periodic table uses *Fe* for the element."

"Maybe he'll grow up to be a scientist like you."

"We can name him Ferruccio if you insist, but I'll be calling him Ferrum." She then babbled the word at the boy in her arms. The boy cocked his head in confusion as she spoke to him. She mispronounced the word with a firm *N* at the end, and he cooed with fascination. "Oh! Do you like *Ferrun*?" The boy grabbed hold of his mother's finger. "Write that down instead, Vito."

His father let out an uncomfortable groan. "I already wrote down Ferruccio," he said, holding the birth certificate up for her to see.

"Hopefully he doesn't inherit your impatience," she said with a laugh. "What a unique name you'll have, my son." She looked down at him, wiggling her finger in his hands.

The finger slipped out of Ferrun's tiny hands. He let a small yawn out of his toothless mouth and closed his eyes to rest.

***

The next morning, Ferrun woke up to a small crowd of people quietly milling around him. Each person stole glances at him, probably wondering when he'd wake up. After a full night's rest, they seemed to have come up with more questions about his story and were now waiting to ask.

Ferrun, who wanted a few more minutes of shut-eye before getting up, felt the curious eyes crawling on his skin. He sat up on his rope pallet and stretched as a few people eagerly greeted him with good mornings.

A man sat down next to him with a smile. "About your story last night… How did you know the world's round? You left the mountain but wound up at it again. When you set off, how did you know you'd end up back here? Did you study the sun and its shadows?" As he asked his questions, a few more people began huddling around Ferrun.

Ferrun looked at the man, still groggy from the night's sleep. "I didn't know about the world being round when I started following my rope."

"You had to have known. Otherwise, why would you give up all the progress of being at the base of the mountain?"

"It was what I had to do," Ferrun said with a shrug.

The man began to ask him another question, or perhaps start an argument, but a woman interrupted him by asking, "What if I follow my rope and wind up in the middle of nowhere next to my rock and don't know how to get back to the mountain?"

Ferrun thought about this while a few other people chimed in with their thoughts. One said, "Going the opposite direction of my rock got me this far. It's supposed to be a guide."

Everyone looked at Ferrun expectantly. He hadn't realized that following his rope would lead him to the mountain. He hadn't even considered the idea that someone might return to their rock and not know where to go next. When Gesa finished her map, she would try to cross the ocean because that's where Ferrun said the mountain was. She wouldn't know she could get there much quicker by land unless her exploration showed her otherwise.

He wondered if Gray was right. He wondered if he'd been leading everyone astray. He felt sweat on his brow as he tried to think of answers to their questions.

"I have an answer." It was the man from yesterday who'd just sat there picking his teeth. He looked at Ferrun as if Ferrun could lend him credibility.

"Of course you have an answer, Rungson," someone in the crowd said.

The man ignored the comment. Ferrun nodded to him, granting him the floor.

"Aside from the fact that we have all eternity to search for the mountain," the man said, "we also will have other people's ropes to follow."

"What if everyone picks up their rope?" someone asked before the man could finish.

Rungson's eyes flared with frustration, but it quickly subsided. "If everyone has picked up their rope and you are the last one, Lysanias, it serves you right for procrastinating that long. I was going to say that there are also patterns in this world. We've all seen it. The forest gets thicker as we get closer to the mountain—"

"What about the ocean?" someone asked. "That's impossible to travel through."

Ferrun began to speak, but someone else spoke first.

"It's not impossible because Ferrun did it."

Lysanias, the man who'd asked the first question of the morning, said, "This whole scheme seems like a good idea if, and only if, you're lucky enough to be tied to the mountain. Unfortunately, that's not a gift the gods have seen fit to bestow on most of us. Turning back to get our rock will put us behind square one because we wouldn't know where the mountain is."

"We need a guiding direction to travel in," someone said.

"Why not the sun like Lysanias suggested?" Ferrun said without much confidence.

"We don't know how to navigate by the sun," Lysanias said.

Rungson rolled his eyes. "Do your knuckles get sore from being dragged on the ground?" Ferrun tried to keep a straight face when someone else snickered. "You have all the time in this world to figure out how to get to the top of that mountain. Use some of it to figure out how to navigate by the sun. It can't be that hard. It rises in the east and sets in the west."

"How do we know that's west?" someone asked.

Rungson let out a heavy sigh and shared a look with Ferrun that seemed to say, "I can only do so much."

"Directions are only relative to themselves," Liyu said. "It could be anywhere as long as it's consistent. What about the boat, Ferrun? How did you know how to build it?"

"What if the sun's not consistent?" a woman asked Liyu before Ferrun could answer the new questions.

"Stop!" Ferrun shouted before the conversation splintered too much.

Everyone halted their bickering and looked at him. Rungson raised an eyebrow.

"I don't know any more than you do," Ferrun explained. "I didn't know the world was round. I didn't know how to build a boat. I didn't know how to knot rope or build a hut in the heat of the desert. They were shots in the dark and friends helped me. It took me a dozen attempts to figure out how to roll the rope up correctly and a dozen more to get it to unravel when I wanted it to. Teekola helped me with that, and his friendship helped me not lose hope throughout my travels.

"I never thought my rock would be the mountain. Honestly, I expected to arrive at my rock and have it be a massive boulder at least the size of a tree. If I had gotten to it and it was truly that big, I would have been in trouble. But someone once told me I was not someone who stays stuck long. If there's any single trait that has served me well, it's that I refuse to stay in one place." He looked at the people in the crowd. Rungson was smiling, but Lysanias glared at Ferrun as if waiting for the right moment to jump in and speak. Ferrun refused to give it to him.

"Collecting my rope was the best way I found to stay unstuck. It wasn't foolproof. No plan is. However, it kept me moving. I am going to carry that sentiment forward and begin climbing the mountain today. I hope all of you adopt the same philosophy in your own way. You don't have to turn back for your rock, but don't stay stuck. I've seen plenty of people stuck in one way or another. Please, don't do the same."

Someone timidly asked, "Won't you at least teach us how to tie our rope in balls like yours?" This made Rungson smile.

Ferrun wanted to say yes. He wanted to walk out of the clearing with each of them and teach them, but it reminded him of his time wandering through the woods, sharing his idea. He didn't want to lose more of the day getting caught up in small questions. "Liyu knows how to do it, and if you don't learn from him, you have an eternity to figure it out on your own. I did it, and so can you."

Lysanias muttered something loud enough for others to hear, but Ferrun missed it. Rungson seemed to have heard it but found it worth ignoring, so Ferrun followed suit.

Ferrun cleaned up his rope pallet and began hiking up the mountain. He let out slack effortlessly, no longer worried whether he was making progress in the right direction.

V

Rock.

Chapter Twenty-Seven

F errun shivered as his bare hands shook and let out rope. Nearly a
week of hiking up the mountain had passed. Each day was colder
than the last. His bare feet, numb from the day's walking, stepped on
something round and strange. He bent over and picked it up.

It was a rope. It was so taut that he could lift it only a few inches
from the ground. It weaved in and out of the thick forest that surrounded him. He looked up, teeth chattering, to judge the distance
between his position and the top of the mountain.

The glimpses he could make of the ascent between the trees didn't
give him much information. Clouds obscured the top of the mountain, and all he knew for sure was that he had a long and cold climb in
front of him. But it would certainly be shorter than the trip he'd taken
to circumnavigate the globe.

He pulled at the taut rope and it barely budged. It weaved between
trees, and he considered following it. It led up the mountain and
followed a trail at least one person could walk. Merc had said years ago
that there were some people on the mountain, but he figured the odds
of meeting them were slim. He dropped the rope and began following
it. He was intrigued by the prospect of talking to someone who'd made
it this far up and was glad to be moving again to fight off the cold.

The rope, lucky for him, wound its way up the mountain in slow and winding paths instead of attacking the steep climb straight on. While he followed it through the dense forest, his rope balls would occasionally get stuck between two trees. At first he could squeeze them through, but after a day of travel, he found himself being more mindful of how he followed the rope trail.

The next morning, Ferrun found a second rope intersecting with the first. After studying the paths of rope, he realized that this second rope seemed to go off on a straight path to follow the first. He suspected someone following Ferrun's rope would see the same pattern where he'd found the first line.

Before the sun went down, taking any remaining warmth with it, the pair of ropes intersected with a third. This one seemed to meet the second rope at a slight angle, and Ferrun couldn't discern which one had gotten there first. As he continued to follow the ropes, his interest increased. He was glad he wasn't the only one curious about others who were successfully scaling the mountain.

He went to bed under a blanket of rope and wondered if he would be the fourth person to make it to the top of the mountain. As his teeth chattered, he wondered why these people followed each other's ropes and wondered if this was the optimal path—and if, with all of his balls of rope, he even needed an optimal path.

***

Ferrun only had to follow the three ropes for the morning before he found where they led to. The forest opened up to a clearing. Stumps littered the open area, indicating it was once as dense as the nearby forest. In the center of the clearing was a small log cabin. Two of the three ropes led through the front door. The other one led around the side of the structure.

Ferrun approached and knocked on the door.

A short woman with a kind face opened the door and looked at Ferrun in shock. Her light purple eyes opened wide. "Heidi, come here. I thought it was strange Arnold was knocking."

A second woman appeared at the door, peeking around the first. She looked younger, and she gawked at Ferrun, looking up and down.

"I'm so excited our family is growing. I always wanted a big family in my life," the purple-eyed woman said.

Not knowing what to do, Ferrun gave them a weak hello.

"Hello to you too," Heidi said. "Come on in. You look like you're freezing."

Ferrun pulled on his rope in just the right way to let out some slack, and he walked into the cabin. He didn't need much, considering the place was only about ten feet on each side. The place was warm, and Ferrun saw a small fire burning in a stone fireplace. The women gestured to a small table with three chairs.

"You can sit in Arnold's spot since he's out right now," the woman with the purple eyes said. "I guess we'll have to make another chair, Heidi." She smiled at Ferrun. "I'm Esmerelda, and I was the second one here."

Ferrun nodded. He wondered which rope she correlated to but was unsure of how to phrase the question. Before he could ask, Heidi set a small clay cup in front of him. It had steaming liquid in it.

"I'm really surprised we didn't hear you coming," Heidi said. "You snuck right up on us. When I arrived, I was third," she added with pride. "Arnold and Es heard me coming a mile away. By the time I was in the clearing, they were able to help me pull in enough slack to get me into the cabin. But not by much." She tugged at the rope on her ankle by moving her leg back and forth. Judging by the amount of rope on the floor, Ferrun didn't think she could make it to the opposite wall from the door. "Isn't it funny how we all got stuck at the same place?" She looked at him with a smile.

Ferrun took a sip of the hot drink in front of him. It tasted like hot water with a bit of mint flavor that cooled the back of his throat.

"It's good, right?" Esmerelda asked. "Heidi makes it with some herbs we grow in the back."

Before Ferrun could answer, the door opened and a man filled the doorway. The man stepped inside and hung a stone ax on the wall. "What on Earth is with all that rope outside?" Once he'd secured the ax in place, he saw Ferrun sitting at the table. Esmerelda and Heidi sat in their spots, smiling with anticipation. "Did you bring all that rope with you?" He loomed over the table. The roof was only a few inches above his head.

"What are you talking about, Arnold?" Esmerelda asked, but before he could answer, she said, "This is—" She paused, and Ferrun figured it was because he hadn't had a chance to introduce himself. She settled on, "Our new cabinmate," then added, "He got here only a few minutes ago. He's the fourth one to reach this high on the mountain!"

"Did either of you look outside at what he brought with him?" Arnold asked.

"He brought a rope behind him," Heidi said, unimpressed. "That's not surprising considering—"

Arnold cut her off by holding up a hand. He opened the door and gestured outside. The cold breeze came in and stirred the fire. "Go look for yourself. I can't explain it."

"Shut that. It's freezing out there," Esmerelda said.

Arnold rolled his eyes in frustration and stepped outside, not shutting the door behind him. Then he reappeared, having to enter sideways because of the large rope ball he had under each arm.

"What on Earth?" Esmerelda said in shock.

Heidi was about to add her own comment, but Arnold spoke first. "There's a few dozen more out there. They're all connected straight to him." He pointed at Ferrun, the stranger sitting in his chair. "I think it's time we had our new guest explain how he got here with this much rope, but he should at the very least tell us his name."

Not sure where to begin, Ferrun took a sip of the minty drink. He then wearily got into who he was and how he found himself on the mountain. He had a feeling these people wouldn't be eager to have someone around who could so easily pass them on the mountain.

Chapter Twenty-Eight

He wrapped up his story talking about the people he'd met at the bottom of the mountain, unable to ascend because of their rocks. When he mentioned this, the people in the cabin showed some satisfaction that they weren't stuck down there.

"So you were clever enough to get yourself tied to the mountain. That's some good thinking," Arnold said after Ferrun had finished.

"Well, I wouldn't say that," Ferrun replied.

Before he could say more, Heidi asked, "How long have you been hiking up the mountain?"

The room grew quiet. They were all eager to hear the answer to this. He realized it had been only a couple of days, so he rounded up and said, "About a month."

"My Lord," Arnold said under his breath while Heidi gasped.

Esmerelda squinted at Ferrun with her purple eyes. "No," she said, "that's not right. You must not be counting your time right."

Ferrun was unsure of how to answer this accusation. "Maybe I'm a little off. Maybe it was two months."

Arnold leaned forward. He'd taken his large chair back, and Ferrun was sitting on one of his rope balls. In a conspiratorial tone he said, "It took me three years to reach this far up the mountain. Es took at least five years by her count. Heidi"—he looked at her and frowned—"she took ten years, and the last year of that was merely getting from the edge of the clearing to the cabin."

Ferrun frowned, knowing that Heidi barely had enough slack to reach the other side of the shelter. He knew there was nothing he could say that would justify his speed, so he sipped more of his mint drink, which had become cold over the course of his story.

"So I guess you won't be staying with us here for long." Esmerelda let the statement hang there as she looked at her companions.

"It is pretty cold out there, so I'm in no hurry to move on," Ferrun said noncommittally. "But, yes, eventually I'll be on my way. I'm not big on being stuck in one place for a long time." He gave them a smile, meaning for it to be encouraging, but he saw the group wasn't amused by the sentiment.

Esmerelda gave him a flat stare, and Heidi refused to look at him. Ferrun felt like his mere existence was causing everyone their discomfort. Not sure what he could add, he sipped on the last of his beverage. The clay cup felt rough on his lips. "You all know everything about me. But I don't know anything about any of you. How did you meet up here?"

Arnold looked at Esmerelda and Heidi, but for once the pair wasn't eager to speak. He took the lead and said, "I was the first one up here. I pulled my rock, which is on the smaller side, behind me and made it to the far edge of the clearing when I got stuck. I was locked in place for over a year, waiting out the cold nights behind some trees. Eventually I decided I'd try to build something to block the wind. I built a little stone ax and began working on this cabin."

"Do you still work on trying to make progress with your rock?" Ferrun asked.

"Every day," the man said with pride. "Although sometimes it's just a light tug as I reach the edge of the clearing. I've been stuck in this spot for almost twenty years by my last count. Trees don't come down quickly with a crummy stone ax, but luckily I've got time. My rock has gotten unstuck twice in all that time. Each time I gained about a yard of slack, maybe less."

Ferrun tried to hide his shock, but he suspected he didn't do a good job of it. He considered the nearly four years he'd spent following his rope around the globe a significant amount of time, but even then he had never stayed in one spot for a whole year, let alone ten of them.

"I'm pretty sure I'm stuck here for good," Arnold continued. "That last bit of slack I got was so long ago I don't remember when it was. I just remember knowing that it happened. Whoever is in charge around here doesn't want me making any more progress."

"I know the feeling," Heidi chimed in from next to the fire. She had gotten up to make more tea for everyone to sip on.

"All in all, I can't complain. It's peaceful up here. I'm sure at the base of the mountain I'd run into a lot of travelers who would pass me. Up here no one passes me. The only people I've met are Es and Heidi."

"And we're so easy to get along with," Esmerelda added with a devilish smile. "I got here maybe five or six years ago. I traveled up the mountain for a while, and I saw smoke coming up from the forest, so I started moving towards it. This was back before I showed Arnold how to make a less smokey fire. He was burning anything and everything he could get his hands on. I don't know how you lived in this place with so much smoke.

"Either way I changed course and began climbing towards the cabin. It was slow progress since my rock kept getting stuck, but I made it. I work on unsticking my rock every once in a while, but what's the point?" She gave Ferrun a light shrug. "I'd just get it stuck again when I tried to go higher. And who knows how much more I have to travel?"

Heidi poured everyone another cup of mint tea and sat down after setting the pot near the fire to stay warm. "You already know everything there is to know about me. I spent ten years struggling up to this cabin. I got here maybe two years ago, but like Es said I spent a year of that merely getting from the edge of the clearing. My rock isn't even that big. I don't know why it gets stuck so often." She frowned and took a small sip of her drink. "I still try getting some slack every morning, but I don't expect it to do much for me. I'd be happy if I could get enough to make it to the far wall of this cabin." The final comment drifted off like smoke in the breeze.

After a moment Arnold added, "So that's us. We've made it the highest up the mountain so far. I know because I've searched around below, looking for other people's rope. I haven't made it around the mountain, so you could say we're the highest hikers on this side, but I'm pretty confident no one has made it this high on the other side either."

Ferrun raised an eyebrow at him, less so because he was impressed and more so because he wanted to make the man think he was impressed.

"I always think it's so strange that we all got stuck in the same place," Esmerelda said.

Arnold rolled his eyes as if he had heard the comment a dozen times, and likely he had. "Es thinks there's some kind of wall or canyon that our rocks are getting stuck on. And that's why we get stuck here."

"Well, it's the only reasonable solution. We're all here in the same spot, aren't we? You must have seen it on your way here." She looked at Ferrun.

Ferrun gave a slight frown, then answered honestly. "I haven't seen anything of the sort. The trees get thicker, but that's about it."

"Besides, everyone's rope is a different length," Arnold added. Ferrun nodded along. "It's got to be something else."

"Have you considered it's because you're comfortable here?" Ferrun asked. They wouldn't be the first people he'd met who were in a place they were comfortable with and not making progress because of it.

"What are you saying?" Heidi asked.

"It sounds like he's saying we've given up," Arnold said in an accusatory tone.

"No, no, no," Ferrun said, holding out his hands. "It's not that. I'm just pointing out what Es said, that if she made any progress, it would just cause more headaches."

"I didn't say we'd given up though," Esmerelda chimed in. "I pull on my rope most days, not that it does much good."

"You just think that since you've got all the slack in the world, you're better than those of us who are working hard to pull our rocks up the mountain," Arnold said. "Not all of us are as lucky as you to have our rope tied to the mountain."

It wasn't the first time someone had labeled Ferrun as lucky. At the beginning of his journey, he couldn't have imagined it ever happening. "Turning back and gathering slack is a reasonable strategy for anyone. I'm not lucky just because I got my rope tied to the mountain. And I never said you gave up. I'm just saying that there's not a lot of incentive for you to keep climbing."

"That's right. There's no point in climbing," Esmerelda said. "We're the highest ones on the mountain."

"Well, we're the highest ones until Ferrun leaves," Heidi said, staring down at her cup of tea.

Arnold's eyes flashed with fury at this realization. Ferrun had felt the aggression rising as the conversation continued, but by the time he decided to act on it, he was too late.

Ferrun jumped off his ball of rope as Arnold bolted across the table. A clay cup shattered. Heidi screamed, and Esmerelda started to ask what was going on. Ferrun got his hand on the door and was going to open it to the outside, where he might have a chance of escaping. As soon as he grabbed it, however, his ankle was stuck and he couldn't move forward. He turned around and saw that Arnold had Ferrun's slack under his foot. The man's massive weight was keeping Ferrun from escaping out the door.

"You're not going to beat us up the mountain!" Arnold shouted.

Ferrun was stuck in front of the door, unable to make it out. Arnold began to make his way towards him, stepping on the rope every bit of the way. Ferrun grabbed the only thing within reach, the stone ax. He swung it wildly, and this stopped Arnold from advancing.

"Let me out!" Ferrun protested. In the chaos, the man hadn't given Ferrun any slack. "I'm not doing any of you any harm by finishing my journey up the mountain."

Arnold laughed a deep laugh. "You're doing us plenty of harm. You're insulting all of our hard work of making it this far by using your trickery. There's no way we're going to let you make it past us."

Ferrun swung the ax in defiance, but it did little good. The two men were at a stalemate. Esmerelda's purple eyes were filled with fury, and Heidi had backed away from the situation as far as her slack would let her.

Arnold bent over and picked up Ferrun's rope.

"Don't!" Ferrun shouted, pointing the ax at the man.

It didn't deter Arnold. The man pulled. Ferrun's weight was nothing compared to the logs he had lugged to build the cabin. Ferrun's feet were pulled out from under him. The world jumped up to him, and his head hit the floor of the cabin. His head throbbed as his vision went black.

***

Ferrun sat at the bar, drinking his third beer that afternoon. He should have been at the office, working on finalizing the research, but after the email he got, he didn't have the heart to figure out how to wrap up the countless loose ends.

Jeremy sat down next to him. "Long said you might be over here."

"He tell you about the email?" Ferrun's words came out quicker than he thought they would.

"He said a few things about it. How are you doing?"

Ferrun gestured at the mostly empty mug. "I've been better."

"You'll be fine," Jeremy insisted. "This stuff happens all the time."

"I'm supposed to be up for review next year. I was going to publish this, and it was going to pay off."

"Publish what you have."

"I don't have anything." Ferrun finished off the beer and waved to the bartender with the eyepatch.

"You've got to have something. You've been on this for years."

"And haven't gotten anything." He tapped on the mug to order another one.

The bartender gave Ferrun a look. His eye turned to Jeremy.

"Let's have some burgers and water instead," Jeremy said. He pulled his friend off the barstool and over to a comfortable booth.

"Why didn't they renew my grant?" Ferrun lamented. He sat lopsided in the booth.

"Times are tough with everything going on."

"Which is why they need this material more than ever."

"I know that. You know that. Dr. Long knows that. Hell, they probably know it too, but money doesn't grow on trees."

"It grows on bushes. Cotton bushes. And they can print more of it if they want."

"It's going to be okay; you can pick up easier research and publish that."

"Who cares if I can make aluminum foil half a micron thinner?"

The motherly server came over to hand them menus, and Jeremy asked for a couple of waters.

"Easy projects need answers too," Jeremy said after the server had left. "Half the studies I cite were slam-dunk tests, but they still needed to be done. And I can name half a dozen studies they thought were straightforward but wound up not going as expected and sprouted whole new fields."

"Really?" Ferrun felt doubtful.

"Well, maybe not whole new fields, but that's why we're testing these things. So we know how the world works."

"I'll tell you how the world works," Ferrun said belligerently.

"Life sucks then you die," Jeremy said to keep the words out of Ferrun's mouth. "But you've got good stuff going for you. You're an uncle. You're healthy. You're alive. After that accident last year, they didn't know if you were going to be able to walk again. Come on, let's order something." He pushed the menu across the table.

"My dad won't stop calling me for money, and we don't talk about anything else. I have nightmares about that little girl, and I just lost funding for the only project I care to work on." Ferrun noticed the menu had a strange design on the cover. It wasn't the one he was used to. He dreaded the thought of opening it.

"There are other projects, and when you have more credentials under your belt, you can reapply."

"If no one solves it by then."

"No one's going to solve it."

"That's what I'm afraid of." Ferrun picked at the corner of the menu.

"That's not what I mean."

Ferrun flipped the menu open, trying to think of something clever to say back to Jeremy. It unfolded, then continued to unfold. His head went dizzy, and the expanding menu encompassed his whole field of view. His world went dark, and it felt like his whole being was being forced to face the discomfort of eternity.

Chapter Twenty-Nine

Ferrun woke up in the dim light of morning. A cloud of vapor appeared every time he exhaled. His fingers and toes were already cold, and he hoped as the sun rose it would warm him up.

Once again, Ferrun was stuck. Arnold, likely with the help of Esmerelda and Heidi, had tied him to the base of a tree on the downhill side of the clearing. They hadn't been gentle about it either. The rope constricted his chest, and there was no wiggling his body one way or the other. Ferrun flexed his hands and wiggled his toes in an attempt to get blood flowing to warm them up.

As the sun rose in the sky behind him, his frustration at his captors grew. He didn't understand why they would work so hard to hold him back. Tying him to a tree wouldn't put them higher up the mountain.

By mid-morning Arnold finally left the cabin. With a smug grin on his face, he approached Ferrun. He'd tied Ferrun in a seated position, and because of that the man towered over him.

"Good morning," Arnold said maliciously. The man squatted to get closer to Ferrun's eye level, but even then the man was still half a head taller. "We tried to do it right this time. Looking back, I think that Gray guy you mentioned had the right idea. Too bad it took too long to catch you. I'm sure there are a lot of people down there taking your crappy advice." He shrugged as if they were no concern to him.

"Hope you're comfortable because I think you're going to be here a long time."

"Why can't you let me go on my way?" Ferrun asked.

"Because you cheated. You're going to make it to the top of the mountain without doing any of the hard work we've had to do."

"I didn't cheat. We had the same opportunity. I've faced just as many challenges as you."

Arnold laughed a deep laugh at this statement. "Don't compare your short jaunt around the world with the decades I've spent fighting my rock to gain even a meter of distance."

"Then turn back!" Ferrun yelled at the man. "If you're so sick of being stuck, then leave. You could have gotten to your rock four times over in all the time you've wasted here."

Arnold stood up and gave Ferrun a thin smile. "No, I don't think I'll be going back. I'm happy here. I've made it higher on the mountain than anyone else. I'm not giving that up on the advice of someone dumb enough to pick a rock he can't move."

"There are a dozen people down there right now collecting rope. They'll be up this mountain soon, maybe not this year, maybe not next year, but they'll be here. They'll beat you to the top, even if you hold me here for eternity."

Arnold shrugged. "I'll believe it when I see it. I'll be surprised if they can figure out how to navigate back to the mountain."

Before Ferrun could say anything, the man walked away. He watched Arnold return to the cabin, grab the stone ax, and disappear to the other side of the clearing.

***

Arnold visited him at least once a day to taunt him. Each time, Ferrun would try to reason with the man and convince him that he wasn't a threat. Arnold had yet to be convinced.

A strange thing that Ferrun noticed was that none of the hikers had attempted to pull on their rope. Not even Heidi, who was so short on slack that she could move through only part of the cabin. He knew they hadn't been pulling on their rope because he could see anyone leaving the cabin, and all the rope ran right next to where he was fastened to the tree.

Arnold was right in that he had done a better job than Gray. Despite a week of attempting to break out of his ropes, Ferrun had made no progress. The only way he would be getting out was if Arnold untied him, and this would require an unlikely change of heart in the big man.

Ferrun hadn't talked to either of the women in the time he'd spent tied to the tree. They'd enter and leave the cabin without a word. Esmerelda spent a lot of time behind the cabin, where they kept the herb garden. Occasionally, he'd seen Heidi leave and come back with clumps of dirt, and he suspected this was clay to remake the cup that was broken in the commotion of his attempted escape.

On a particularly cold morning, Ferrun woke up from a shallow sleep at the sound of the cabin door shutting. It was quieter than normal, but he'd grown used to the sound that would come before one of Arnold's scoldings. He didn't see the big man approaching. Instead, he saw Heidi carrying something in her hands.

She came and knelt down next to him, and he could see that she held a clay cup of tea. "Here, I thought you might be cold this morning," she said in a hushed tone. She lifted the cup to his mouth, and he sipped the drink carefully.

It was steaming hot, and the warmth in his chest was soothing. He had barely slept that night, or any of the nights since being tied to the tree. He thanked her for the tea.

"I'm really sorry." Her tone sounded guilty as if she had done the whole thing herself without anyone else's help or input.

"Why'd you do it?" Ferrun asked.

"I didn't do it. Arnold did. He said you were a threat to us."

Ferrun nodded. He'd heard every single excuse the man could make. "I meant why did you bring me tea?"

"Oh," she said, embarrassed, "I was cold, and I couldn't sleep. Everyone else was out, so I made some tea for myself. Then I saw the extra cup and thought you might like some as well. You haven't been sleeping well out here, have you?"

"I look that bad?" Ferrun couldn't see himself, but he suspected he had heavy bags under his eyes, and his hair and face were a mess from not being able to wipe away any dirt that he'd kicked up.

"Yeah, you do look that bad," Heidi said somberly.

Ferrun shrugged. "You don't think I'm going to get untied anytime soon, do you?" He already knew Arnold's position on the matter.

"No," Heidi said in a still tone. She lifted the cup up to his mouth, offering more tea, and Ferrun sipped the last of the drink.

When he was done with the cup, he said, "You could always untie me." His tone conveyed more hope than he expected for how unlikely it was to happen.

Heidi frowned at the comment, unwilling to make eye contact with Ferrun. Without saying anything, she got up and went back into the cabin.

Ferrun was left with a fading warmth in his belly from the tea and a lot of questions about Heidi's motivations and ideals.

After an hour passed, Arnold was back in front of Ferrun, telling him how hopeless he was while tied to the tree. Ferrun couldn't disagree with the man since his only chance of escape was merely willing to bring him a hot beverage.

***

"You're not the first person I've met who's not from Earth," Ferrun told Heidi. It was a cold night, and they'd finished their tea a while ago. The two were quietly recounting their memories of their lives in the dark.

"That makes sense. Once humanity spread past their home solar system, a majority of humans wouldn't have lived on Earth. Meaning the majority of humans in the afterlife wouldn't be from Earth."

"And what about the aliens? Where are they in this afterlife?"

"I'm not sure where they were in my mortal life. We found basic life such as microbes everywhere, but anything more complicated than a lizard was unheard of. Intelligent species like humans were rare, and mostly just legends."

"That's terrifying," Ferrun said with a shiver.

"Just a fact of life," Heidi said, pulling some of Ferrun's rope balls around her to block out the wind.

"And what did you do on this colony planet you lived on?"

"Ordered food."

"Like pizza delivery?"

"What's pizza delivery?"

"The job that got me through college," Ferrun said with a laugh. "Someone takes a pizza from the shop it's cooked at and delivers it to your door."

"How long does that take? Wouldn't it get cold?"

"It takes thirty minutes or less or it's free."

"Thirty minutes from ordering food to getting it to your door?! How's it not disgusting by then?"

"Where did you order food from?"

"The Central System, specifically the Omarian Conglomerate. They made the foodcrowave and the ingredients it needed to make food."

"Foodcrowave? Like a microwave?"

Heidi stifled a laugh. "It's a robot that can instantly make anything you order. Everyone had one in their home, and most workplaces had it in their break room. We all got food nearly instantly after ordering it."

"Cooked by a robot?" Ferrun didn't know if that was the kind of food he'd want to eat. "Was it any good?"

"Better than any homecooked meals people could make. Those who knew how to cook were rare. The most I can make is tea."

"My ancestors would be rolling in their graves if I never learned how to cook. If all the cooking was done for you, what did you have to order?"

"With over half a million people on the colony and at least a million foodcrowaves, I had to keep everything in stock while managing expenses. Food was still a commodity, and prices fluctuated. Also, it took time to ship it across the galaxy to us."

"What about everyone else in there?" Ferrun said, nodding as best he could to the cabin despite his bound state.

"They're both from Earth like you. Es is from before the moon landing. She still doesn't believe Arnold and me when we say it happened. She always wanted a family, but there were complications in that plan, so she volunteered and worked with kids a lot."

"And Arnold?" Ferrun asked. "What sweet thing did he do to earn his place in the afterlife?" He remembered his conversation with Hazel and still doubted that virtuous actions had gotten him here. Still, it was hard finding a redeeming quality in someone who tied you to a tree.

"He had a tough life," Heidi said quietly. "He had a lot of jobs. Never could hold them down. One accident after another followed him. He had an office job but got laid off because someone higher up mismanaged funds. Then he worked as a bus driver but ran a guy over. This was before they had perfected self-driving cars. He lost that job but didn't go to jail at least. Then he was pretty depressed, not that I can blame him, and he worked odd jobs here and there."

"No kidding," Ferrun wondered if anyone would believe the coincidence of him dying by being hit by a bus. "How'd he die?"

"He never said, but his dreams are restless, so I can't imagine it was peaceful. He thinks hard work is what got him here." Heidi yawned. "From what I've seen, he's nothing short of a hard worker."

"Even clearing this area with a stone ax was a feat," Ferrun said. He'd cut down a number of trees to make his boat and knew it wasn't an easy task.

"I've got to go to sleep," Heidi said, picking up the clay cups.

"You sure you don't want to untie me first?" Ferrun said with a smile.

"I'm sorry," Heidi said. "Arnold wouldn't let me back into the cabin if I did that."

"Worth a shot," Ferrun said with a yawn. He was tired, but he knew it'd be a fitful sleep tied up to the tree.

Chapter Thirty

The door of the cabin cracked open, and Heidi slipped out into the dim light of the morning. It was beginning to happen every few mornings. She would bring Ferrun some warm tea, and they would talk or just sit together in silence.

Ferrun pointlessly wiggled his toes. Days ago, he'd resigned himself to having his feet constantly fall asleep from the precarious position he sat in under the tree. He knew all four of them were stuck on the side of the mountain, but somehow he felt he had more in common with Heidi than the others. She knelt down next to him and held the cup of tea to his lips.

When he was finished with his first small sip of the hot beverage, he asked, "What does Esmerelda think about all this?" He nodded to the tree he was tied to.

Heidi shrugged and said, "I think she's fairly indifferent. She isn't as competitive as Arnold is, but she likes to keep him happy. I think she's grateful he built the cabin and all; otherwise, she would just be stuck out in the cold."

"And that would be awful," Ferrun said dryly.

"Sorry," Heidi said meekly.

Ferrun smiled at her. "I'd say it's not a big deal, but it sucks. I just can't blame you for it."

"I should have stopped him." It was a point that she brought up often.

"What were you going to do?" Ferrun scoffed. "Tie him to the tree? He's twice your size."

"I could have tried to talk him out of it," she said, but she seemed unconvinced of herself.

"I've worked that angle for months now. It's not likely to work. Short of someone else deciding to untie me, I don't think I'm going anywhere soon." He often made a point of mentioning being untied when Heidi was around. He worried it put him in jeopardy of not getting tea anymore, but it didn't seem to change Heidi's habits.

"If I untied you, I'd be stuck here with Arnold mad at me after you've escaped. He would know it was me."

"You wouldn't be stuck here."

"What am I going to do? Run away up the mountain with you? I can't even reach halfway across this clearing."

"You could go down the mountain," Ferrun suggested. His body shook from either the excitement or the cold. He couldn't tell which.

"Arnold could still find me if he wanted to."

"He could, but I don't think he'd be willing to lose ground on the mountain to find you."

"He's a complicated man."

"How so?" Ferrun asked. To him, the man simply seemed vengeful.

"He thinks the hard work of his life is what earned him his trial. Your easy ascent up the mountain undermines that."

Ferrun began formulating an explanation about how his hard journeys have been, but the door of the cabin slamming open cut him off. In the early morning sun, Ferrun could see the silhouette of Arnold. A shiver shot down his spine like a thunderbolt. He looked to where

Heidi had stood, but she'd disappeared. Arnold lumbered his way to Ferrun's tree and looked down at him.

"What were you two talking about?" The man spat the question at Ferrun like he deserved an answer. Arnold checked the woods, looking for Heidi.

Ferrun responded to the man's question by saying, "The architectural subtleties that you built into the cabin."

Arnold kicked him in the gut. "Was she untying you?" He inspected Ferrun's knots.

"She actually untied me weeks ago. I was just so comfortable here that I decided to stay." He didn't hear anything from Heidi, and as far as he could tell, Arnold couldn't see her in the thick forest. The three ropes that used to run next to him leading into the clearing were now only two.

Arnold tightened Ferrun's already restrictive bonds, then shouted into the woods. "You better not come back, traitor!"

Unsure of where she'd gone, Ferrun said, "She went to go get her rope. She's going to get to the top of the mountain before you, whether you like it or not."

Arnold spat in Ferrun's direction, but the wind took the projectile off its course. He then returned to the cabin and began his daily routine of chopping wood.

Ferrun couldn't see any of the woods behind him but kept listening for sounds of Heidi. He hoped she had taken his advice and started searching for her rock down the mountain. He just wished she'd had the time to untie him during her escape. Now it was too risky for her to pull it off since Arnold would be on the lookout for her.

Around midday Esmerelda came out of the cabin and called for Arnold. Ferrun couldn't hear what they were talking about at first, but as the conversation went on, it grew heated. When they got to shouting, he could hear bits and pieces, including "Heidi," "traitor," "abandoned," "how could you," and "helpless." The argument went on for hours, and eventually Esmerelda retreated to the cabin, slamming the door behind her. Arnold tried to follow her, but the door was barred shut to even his strength.

Ferrun snickered at the idea of Arnold being locked out of his own cabin. Unfortunately, the man then turned his frustration to Ferrun. He walked across the clearing to his place of captivity.

"Look what you've done," the man proclaimed in an unforgiving voice.

Ferrun turned his head side to side in what he thought was a comical gesture. It earned him a kick in the ribs, and he thought he felt something break.

"Everything was fine before you came along. Then you had to sow seeds of uncertainty in everyone's mind." Arnold hoisted the ax in anger. "I ought to kill you just to see if any of your story is true. You said we couldn't die. Want to see if you can return from a beheading?"

Ferrun looked at the ax and had a feeling the man could do it, but it would likely take a couple of rather uncomfortable swings.

"Nothing clever to say to that?"

Ferrun swallowed, trying to keep his fear of the situation hidden.

The man seemed content with his accomplishment of making Ferrun afraid. He kicked dirt in his face before returning to chop wood.

When the sun began to set, Arnold returned to the cabin, but the door was still barred. He shouted at it, as well as the woman inside, for a while, but when night fell, the man was stuck outside in the cold.

Ferrun was grateful that it was too dark for the man to navigate to him because whatever anger the man had stored up would likely be detrimental to Ferrun's already aching chest. Soon Arnold's snores echoed into the night, and Ferrun wished he could get the same restful sleep.

***

Ferrun found he'd gotten some sleep because he was startled awake by someone shaking him lightly on the shoulder. The early morning light barely illuminated the woman next to him.

"I'm sorry I left," Heidi said. "I just didn't want to deal with him."

"Why'd you even come back?" he asked. The light was too dim for him to see Arnold or the cabin, but he heard the man's snores travel across the early morning air.

"To untie you. You shouldn't be stuck here with him. He's gone crazy."

Ferrun agreed with the statement as Heidi began to tug at his knots. She wasn't very good at figuring out how to untie them, and he doubted that the lack of light helped. If the situation were reversed, he figured he'd messed with enough rope and knots that he could get it done quickly.

As the sun rose and brought more light, he felt his bonds get looser. Unfortunately, the more light there was, the more likely Arnold would wake up. His snores still echoed through the clearing for now.

"I can't get this last one," Heidi said after she had pulled at it for a while.

By now the clearing was mostly in full sun, and Ferrun expected Arnold to wake at any moment. "Can you get it a little looser?"

"Maybe."

Ferrun felt the bonds pull hard against his chest, then loosen a little. He wiggled against them, and he could tell he was almost free. He rotated his body a little and saw the knot that Heidi was untying. It was a mess of a thing. Carefully, he wrapped one hand in a strange position to get at the knot and start pulling. "Hold that line there," he told Heidi as he pointed with his finger. "No, the other one. Perfect."

He tugged against them for a minute and began to make progress. Then Heidi said in a small tone, "Uh-oh."

Ferrun's mind went frantic as his ears registered what was wrong. Arnold's snores had stopped. Ferrun began to frantically pull at the knot, still making slow progress.

"He's coming towards us," Heidi said, and he could tell her focus was drifting away from the knot he was untying.

He wiggled his body some more, and it was enough to get his other hand to the knot. With both hands on the task, he no longer had to guide Heidi through helping him. "Run," he told her.

"What about you?" she asked quietly. Her voice was almost drowned out by Arnold's frustrated screams.

"Just leave," he told her, trying to focus on the knot in front of him.

He could tell by the volume of the man's cursing that he was almost there. Ferrun pulled at the knot and was close to loosening it when his upper arm exploded in pain. He cried out and lost control of some of the fingers he was using to untie the knot. He pulled with his good arm and was able to roll free of the tree. His body was tangled in ropes, and he lay on his back, looking up at Arnold, who towered above him with the ax raised above his head.

The ax's edge was painted red, and Ferrun knew it had something to do with the pain in his arm. As Arnold brought the ax down towards Ferrun, a small projectile flew through the air and connected with the man's head. Stunned, Arnold looked around, and this gave Ferrun an opportunity to clamber out of the way.

"You traitor!" Arnold cried into the forest.

Ferrun crawled into the clearing, putting himself between Arnold and the cabin. It was hard for him to stand up at first, and he realized it was because he was trying to lift himself with the hand he'd lost control of. He finally used his good arm to stand up. The ax had cut his arm to the bone. The ligaments and nerves that controlled the dexterity of his fingers were ruined.

Ferrun couldn't see Heidi in the woods, and he didn't think Arnold could either. Before the man got the nerve to search for her, Ferrun shouted, "She's not the one who's going to beat you up the mountain today."

This got Arnold's attention and he rushed Ferrun. With his good hand, Ferrun dragged his slack and the rope balls that were connected to them and darted through the clearing up the mountain. The man was gaining on him as he passed the cabin. Esmerelda had come out in the noise and confusion and made a grab at Ferrun's slack. He pulled it out of her reach, unable to do much with only one arm.

Ferrun looked over his shoulder as he passed the small garden the hikers had built and saw that Arnold was only a few yards away and closing. He pushed himself as hard as he could but knew the man would catch him soon. He'd be back tied to the tree, and if Heidi was smart, she would be at the base of the mountain, collecting her rope instead of trying to untie him again.

Then he noticed where the trees were thick again, and he realized they hadn't been cut down because Arnold couldn't reach them. He made a mad dash to get to them. Soon he was surrounded by a few stumps. Beyond the stumps was the shade of the untouched forest. Ferrun turned around and saw Arnold at the end of his rope.

Arnold screamed in rage. Ferrun's eyes followed his own rope and saw that there were still some rope balls near the man's feet. He began to reel them in with his good arm. He had to keep them out of reach.

In anger, Arnold threw his ax at Ferrun. It hit a tree instead and stuck there. Ferrun knew that if it had been his chest, he'd be facing the dark void right now. He pulled his last rope ball to the safety of the trees.

Arnold began to curse at Ferrun and tug at his own rope for extra slack. Ferrun figured this was the first time the man had given his rope any real effort in a long time. As the man wrestled with his rope, Ferrun ran a circle around a tree.

Safe from the man's physical attacks, Ferrun held his numb arm. Arnold was still slinging insults at him, but those were harmless. Arnold glared at Ferrun with sheer anger in his eyes, but he looked worn out.

Ferrun pulled the ax out of the tree with his good hand.

Arnold's demeanor changed when he realized what had happened. "Give that back and I'll let you go," he pleaded, his eyes now full of fear of having lost the high ground.

"You couldn't stop me if you wanted to."

Arnold made a dash for Ferrun's slack and began to pull at it. He tried to drag Ferrun off his feet again. The circle Ferrun had made around the tree kept the man from reeling him in.

Ferrun walked towards him anyway with the ax hanging in his good hand. He stopped a yard away from Arnold, who'd pulled his own rope the furthest it could reach. He held the ax out. It was just inches away from the man's grip.

"Give it to me. It's our only source of heat for the cold nights."

Ferrun looked into his eyes—eyes that had filled in turn with anger and fear. Gone was the anger that had looked down at Ferrun for months as he sat tied to the tree in the cold. He could swing the ax at the man and injure him, but he knew a wound would just heal in the morning. Ferrun swung the ax as hard as he could, and it sank deep into the trunk of an unmarked tree.

Arnold's eyes now filled with longing as he reached for the ax. It was only a foot away, but his slack wouldn't let him reach it. Ferrun smirked at him and turned, leaving the man and his curses in the distance.

Chapter Thirty-One

Ferrun's thin linen shirt flapped in the wind as his foot crushed the surface layer of ice that covered the soft snow. He'd left the tree line weeks ago and found himself in a constant battle against wind, snow, and ice. He dragged his balls of rope up the mountain, putting more foot-sized holes into the snow. There was no doubt they'd be filled within the hour.

Looking back at his rope balls, a habit he'd formed to make sure they weren't caught on trees, he noticed there were only a few behind him. He pulled on them, and more emerged from the haze of the snowfall. With all of his rope accounted for, Ferrun turned back to continue his hike. A gust of wind suddenly picked up, and he was blown off his feet and into a snow drift.

Ferrun's teeth chattered, and it was a constant noise he heard in the back of his mind. He pulled his rope balls towards him to make sure they weren't caught on anything. Once they surrounded him in the snowdrift, his body was protected from the wind.

He untangled the rope ball that was closest to his ankle. He hadn't touched it in years, as it was the first rope he'd collected at the base of the mountain. He untangled the ball and wrapped his body in the rope. He had to stand up and brave the cold to wrap his legs, but the more rope he put on, the more protected he felt. He wrapped his chest in layers of rope and felt he would soon look like a rope ball himself. He didn't care. It protected him from the icy wind more than his thin linens. This felt like the most ridiculous thing he'd done with the rope since diving to untangle it from the ocean's depths.

He used the last of the rope ball to wrap his head up. He left a small slit for his eyes, not that he could see much in the blizzard he was facing. He also left a hole for his mouth, but he wrapped his tender ears loosely, worried they were about to freeze off.

He was a man covered in rope, and if anyone else saw him, they'd think he was crazy. Ferrun didn't care. The warmth made it worth it. He faced the white storm through the eye slit and looked for the direction he thought was up.

It didn't take long for him to realize that looking for a direction to go wouldn't work in this storm. He poked around in the cold snow with his wrapped foot to feel for where the ground was higher. As he turned in circles, he thought he found an angle with a subtle difference between the height of the ground beneath each foot. He shifted his weight and repeated the process. He felt for the uphill direction. Once he found it, he took another step.

The process wasn't fast, and the blizzard threw him off balance more than once. Every time he got up, he had to recalibrate to the incline of the mountain. The sky grew dim as he traveled, and he was unsure whether this was nightfall or just the storm getting worse. Not wanting to find out, he untangled some rope and made a pallet for himself on the snow. He buried himself in rope, hoping it would hold his warmth better than the wet and icy snow. Exhausted from the day's fight against the weather, Ferrun fell asleep.

***

Ferrun stood looking at his mother's gravestone. There was another one nearby but without his father's name on it. Vito approached and put a set of flowers on each. He said a prayer, crossing himself at the end.

"You two were probably the best thing that ever happened to me," he said, fighting something in the back of his throat. "You were both too good for an accountant who couldn't manage his money."

Vito took a big sigh and muttered something in Italian, which Ferrun had never learned despite his father's best efforts.

"I got a degree. I'm catching up to you, Ferrun." He cracked a smile, but it soon faded. "Mateo flew in, and the grandkids got all dressed up. I think he was going to stop by. I don't know if he did. Anyway, it puts me up for a promotion. I'll probably be there for only a few more years before retirement, but Jimmy says I'm a shoo-in with my experience. He says if they don't offer it to me, he'll write me a recommendation for a new company his friend is starting."

The man lost the battle with the thing in his throat for a minute. He gained his composure by muttering a few lines about saints.

"I hope you two are doing well, wherever you are. Hope the christening was enough to get you in, Ferrun. Susan, you were an angel here on Earth. At the very least, I hope you know that I'm doing well. Despite all evidence you saw of the contrary. I finally took on a challenge." He muttered some more Italian and said a prayer, crossing himself before climbing into the old car that once looked so new.

Ferrun stared at his mother's grave and read the words he'd picked out with his father a lifetime ago. The dates weren't as close together as the gravestone next to hers, but it still felt like too short a time.

Ferrun wandered away towards the parking lot before realizing he hadn't driven there. He sat down on a bench near a mausoleum that overlooked a small pond, waiting for whatever brought him here to carry him off.

***

Darkness surrounded him when he awoke. Thinking it was the middle of the night, Ferrun attempted to return to sleep. Cold but no longer exhausted to the point of being unable to continue, he realized he had slept all he could, middle of the night or not. He waited for the sun to come up, but it didn't.

Impatient he sat up and broke through the snow that had covered his rope fort. White daylight blinded him, and a gust of wind whipped past his head and whistled through the rope mask he had made. He ducked back behind his barricade. Snow was falling from the sky at sharp angles, and all he could see was the blizzard around him.

He felt around on the ground, compacting the snow to try to find the uphill direction. Every time his body emerged from the snowbank, he was pelted by wind and ice despite his rope's protection. He found it was easier to tell which way was uphill if he lay down. He tunneled through the deep snow towards the peak.

The storm outside continued through the day and night, and Ferrun was constantly exhausted from having to keep himself warm. He tunneled through the snow, finding that if he popped up to take a look around, he would only be buffeted by snow, and it wouldn't give him any hints on which way to go. He used his body as a gauge to know which way to travel. The storm grew worse every day, and lying down was his only indication he was headed up an incline.

Chapter Thirty-Two

F errun lost track of time inside the snow tunnel he built. He slept
when he felt too tired to continue. He poked small holes in his
ceiling to check the time of day and the storm's temperament. After
what felt like months of travel but by the count of his unraveling rope
balls had been only a few weeks, Ferrun poked his head out of the
tunnel to find that the storm had subsided.

Blue sky surrounded him, and he felt the full strength of the sun's
light. He held an arm up to block the light that came from the sky and
reflected off the snow. He observed his surroundings and saw a vast
fog below him. It stretched to the horizon in every direction, making it
look like he was only a few dozen yards from the base of the mountain.
It was the massive storm he had just spent weeks crawling through.
Ferrun had broken through the cloud line.

He turned around, putting his back to the storm, and saw in front
of him the tip of the mountain. It was less than a day's travel away, and
he felt he could reach out and touch it. It was white and serene against
the clear blue sky.

The air was silent. The wind no longer whistled against his ears.
The peak was silent, so he began clapping his hands together to fill the
world with sound. Realizing that the sound might cause the snow to

lose its precarious grip on the mountainside and push him back down into the storm, Ferrun stopped clapping.

The world around him was silent again. He stared at the tip of the mountain, wondering if he was the first one to set eyes on it, or the hundredth. Either way it was a beautiful sight.

The silence around him disappeared once more. He heard the crunch of snow underfoot. He looked down at his own feet, wondering if they had begun moving towards the peak on their own accord, but they remained in the burrow he'd made in the snow.

Ferrun scanned the horizon and quickly saw what was making the sound. His blood began to pump when he saw a brown speck on the horizon. Someone moved towards him, carefully looking down at their own feet and occasionally scanning the horizon as though searching for something.

Only Ferrun's torso was exposed, and he quickly ducked into the protection of the tunnel. He wasn't eager to run into another traveler looking to hold him back from reaching the peak he was now so close to.

After a few minutes, he peeked his head up to gauge how far away the traveler was. It was always easy to find the person since they were the only brown thing in the world at the top of the mountain. Ferrun knew he had equally poor camouflage and only poked his head out for as little time as needed.

He waited and hoped the person would move on to traveling to the top of the mountain, but they seemed intent on continuing their search. Ferrun thought he would be willing to take second place in the trip to the top if it meant he didn't have to deal with another egomaniac's attempt to delay his progress.

The person didn't give up the search and, worse, was getting closer. For the whole afternoon, Ferrun hid in place as the person drew closer.

He checked less often, and each time he did, the brown blotch had grown in size. Soon he could make out that the person had more brown splotches dragging behind them. It took Ferrun a moment to realize that these were balls of rope. At the end he could see a blurry gray dot that had to be the person's rock.

Ferrun considered this. Hiding in his small snow burrow, he weighed his options. Despite his hope that the traveler would be a friend—it was someone open to the idea of following their rope after all—Ferrun still didn't want to trust them so close to the finish line. He considered continuing to burrow to the top just to avoid the person, and it seemed like a reasonable plan. The only problem with burrowing was that the snow was getting more compact and harder to dig through. The sun had likely melted and refrozen so much snow that the tip of the mountain was more ice than snow.

Ferrun poked his head out, and the person was close but had their back turned. They were pulling their rock behind them, and Ferrun could clearly count ten rope balls. The person was tall and broad-shouldered. Ferrun almost thought it was Arnold but realized this person was even bigger. As they began to turn around, Ferrun ducked into his hideout, crunching some icy snow in the process.

"Hello?" the person called out. It was a man's voice.

In the vast silence of the mountaintop it sounded familiar. Ferrun suspected it could be someone he'd met long ago because he had rope balls, but he also knew there were people who collected their rope despite having never met him.

"Hello? Is anyone here?" the man called out into the still world. He crept closer with every shout.

When the voice seemed to be coming from next to him, Ferrun swallowed hard and forced himself to face the inevitable. The icy air went down like a shot of whiskey but didn't give him the confidence he had hoped for. He stood up, and his head poked out of the snow. He prepared to confront the stranger.

The man was surprised by Ferrun's sudden appearance, and it would have given Ferrun an advantage if the person hadn't been just a foot away. Startled, they both jumped back and fell into the snow. Ferrun scrambled to his feet, but the other man was slow to get up.

Carefully setting his feet on the compacted icy snow, Ferrun was ready to pounce as he asked, "Who are you?"

The man, who had only made it to a sitting position, put his hands up in surrender and said, "I don't want to hurt you, friend."

Ferrun still couldn't place the voice, and the man's face and entire body were covered in rope, much like his. He was still poised to attack, although in the back of his mind he knew he would lose if it came to wrestling the large man in front of him.

"I'm Captain Teekola, friend. Who are you?"

Ferrun's body didn't know what to do when he heard the name. He almost didn't believe it, but it wasn't the most unlikely thing he'd experienced. "Captain Isaac Teekola?" He relaxed his weak attempt at an offensive position.

"Is there another one?" Teekola asked.

"It's Ferrun. I can't believe it's you." He pulled away the rope that was protecting his face as if to prove he was who he said he was.

The Captain pulled away the rope that was covering his own face. His brown skin and cropped hair were a comforting and familiar sight to Ferrun. The two men embraced each other, and the warmth Ferrun felt was also comforting.

"What are you doing up here?" Teekola asked.

Ferrun gestured to the top of the mountain. "The same as you, I suppose."

"I thought you would have been up here long ago," Teekola said, amazed.

"I could say the same about you. Boy, do I have some stories to tell you."

"Me too," Teekola echoed.

Ferrun felt the wind pick up and brush against his face, but it was a light breeze compared to the blizzard he had faced. "Let's find a way out of this cold and talk."

Teekola nodded in agreement, wrapping his face back up with the rope. Ferrun hopped into the tunnel he had burrowed in the snow. He packed down the walls, making the space inside bigger to accommodate his friend. When it was ready, Teekola gave himself some slack and climbed down out of the wind.

He looked back at Ferrun's ropes, which were blocking the tunnel in the other direction, and asked, "How many did you wind up with?"

"Over thirty," Ferrun said, wondering if Teekola would believe him.

"And your rock. How big is it? I knew you'd find a way to move it." Teekola removed his rope mask again.

"I never figured out how to move it. We're actually sitting on it." Ferrun patted the ground as he said this.

"What?" Teekola's eyes expanded with surprise.

"My rock turned out to be the mountain. I guess it was the biggest thing they had."

Teekola was shocked by this statement, and then Ferrun saw his face slowly relax as all the pieces fell into place in his mind. "You were moving away from it when we met. Did you travel in a circle?"

"In a way," Ferrun said. "I apparently walked all the way around the globe. It will really only make sense if I tell you the whole story."

Teekola nodded, and through the day and night the men talked about Ferrun's adventures as they sat inside the protection of the small icy burrow.

Chapter Thirty-Three

After Ferrun had finished, Teekola explained that he had found his rock less than a year after they'd split paths. "I wasn't sure if you had reached the top yet, so I decided to spend some time traveling in the forest, meeting others, and telling them about following their rope. I had the same problem as you. Many weren't very receptive despite me having my rock behind me. But a few listened, and I'm sure they will be up here shortly."

Ferrun nodded, wondering why Teekola had decided to wait.

"I think I even found the ocean you crossed," Teekola continued. "Although I just assumed it was the edge of the world. With no need to cross it, I slowly made my way back towards the mountain. I continued to explain things to people, and my fast progress encouraged them more. As I got closer to the mountain, I heard rumors of a rope that was knotted to the side of the mountain, but I never thought it was yours. People are always looking for something to talk about here."

"I didn't believe it was mine either," Ferrun said with a smile, remembering how he had doubted Liyu's claim.

"I guess I came up near the same spot as you since I was hearing about the knot, but I never saw it for myself. I'm glad you finally made it up here. I can't believe how long it took you though."

"Me neither," Ferrun said, recounting the years he had spent traveling.

The sun had begun to rise, and the early morning light seeped into the dark burrow.

"You should probably start heading towards the top once the light is up," Teekola said.

"Yeah, we should." Ferrun was glad he would be summiting with an old friend.

"No, just you. I will wait a day, then follow. You are the only reason I made it this far."

Ferrun looked at the man, puzzled. "You don't have to wait. We can go at the same time. I'm sure it won't be an issue. Besides, you did as much work as I did to get up here."

Teekola laughed a deep laugh at this comment. "I don't think anyone has done as much work as you. You should be the first one up there since I'm here only because of you, and it sounds like you will be the reason many more will make it up here."

Ferrun blushed, embarrassed by how much credit Teekola gave him. After arguing with him for the better part of the morning, Ferrun realized that Teekola was the more stubborn one.

By the time the sun was shining straight down into the burrow, Ferrun conceded that he would go up the mountain first. He gave the big man a hug. Since neither of them knew what was going to happen at the top, they didn't know if they would see each other again. Despite this, they promised each other that if they could meet again, they would.

Ferrun's progress up the mountain went quicker than he expected. When he reached the top, the light of the sun hadn't even diminished. As he stood at the peak, looking out at all the clouds below him, he realized he couldn't find the sun. The light seemed to be coming from everywhere at once. The cold of the mountain faded away, and he felt like he had thawed out.

***

From seemingly nowhere, a man wearing a Hawaiian shirt and bearing a childish smile stood in front of Ferrun.

"Congratulations," Merc said.

He was joined by two others in less brightly colored clothes. One wore a toga and held a staff that was crooked like a lightning bolt, while the other wore fur, had a long beard, and an eye that was patched shut. They both gave him a smile and nodded their heads in congratulations.

"What now?" Ferrun asked. He'd heard almost every theory of what would happen when people got to the top, and he finally accepted the fact that he'd experience it.

The man with one eye stepped forward. "Now you've ascended."

Ferrun nodded. He'd ascended the mountain for days and was wondering what this guy's point was.

"No, it's not just that you've ascended the mountain," the man with the crooked staff said. "Wod means that you've ascended to godhood."

"Godhood?" Ferrun said, confused. "You mean like I'm immortal?"

"You've been immortal since we brought you here," Merc said. "What we're offering you—well, more like forcing upon you—is the opportunity to commune with the fabric of reality in a way you have never done before."

"Commune with the fabric of reality?" Ferrun was now even more confused.

Wod, the bearded man, sighed a heavy sigh and stepped towards Ferrun. Out of nowhere, he produced a spear, and before Ferrun could react, Wod jammed it into Ferrun's chest.

Ferrun reached for the pain, but his vision and senses faded fast. He felt himself fall to the ground, but the impact seemed like nothing to him.

The men were speaking above him, and the one in the toga said, "You could have warned him."

Wod replied with, "It's faster this way, and he'll understand more than we can explain."

Ferrun's senses disappeared after this. He was surrounded by the dark void, the one he'd faced a dozen times over. There was nothing and there was everything. His consciousness was pulled in every direction. He knew, from many experiences before, that he could never fill it. His mind expanded, painfully reaching for the void's nonexistent edges.

He didn't reach the top of the mountain just to suffer through the void once again, he thought. He reached the top of the world because he went about the problem completely differently from everyone else, yet infinity was still going to swallow him up.

Ferrun refused to let it happen. Instead of letting himself disperse, he worked to hold himself together. Fighting against the void, he pushed himself orthogonally towards reality. In return, it pushed him in a direction he didn't know existed.

He no longer encompassed the endless void but looked down upon it fully. The darkness faded, and he saw countless worlds and knew each person in them. Then he knew every animal, every plant, and eventually every molecule. The entirety of everything settled in his mind. He didn't know how he could hold it in his mind at first, then he understood how it worked. He knew everything there was to know and so much more.

Instead of his mind scattering to the edges, he could now look upon everything in time and space. He began to explore the worlds, leaving bits of his consciousness as anchors into the many worlds he saw. Content by his exploration, which took no time in this place outside of time, he projected himself in front of the gods on the mountain.

Standing in front of Merc, looking at his colorful Hawaiian shirt, Ferrun smiled. Wod still had his spear, and he used it to jab at Ferrun again. Ferrun manipulated his being to let the spear pass through, and he was unharmed.

"Quick learner," the man said under his beard.

The god in the toga—Ferrun had since learned his name was Sues—said, "It seems you've got the hang of all this."

Ferrun nodded. He was an astral projection of his former consciousness. He'd integrated with the universe, and instead of being dispersed into the infinity to be reused by other consciousnesses, he'd held himself together.

"You created this world so I could have a chance to ascend," Ferrun said to the group.

The three gods nodded in unison.

"We nurtured your consciousness from your mortal death into this world, where you could experience immortality and the expanse of reality," Merc said.

"That's the void," Ferrun said.

"Most mortals show no promise in their ability to ascend, and we let their consciousness go back into the universe to be used by future life. But you, and all the others in this world, showed something in your lives that indicated you *might* be capable of more."

The dreams he'd had and the haunting nightmares he'd faced in his death clicked together in his mind—various realities that happened or could have happened. "I merely saved a young girl from being hit by a bus," Ferrun said, knowing countless other people across all the worlds that had done that or something greater.

"You took on the impossible task of bringing the child to safety, not knowing how it would end for you," Sues said.

"It didn't end well for you," Merc said. "You were in the news for almost a whole week."

"It was a vain attempt," Wod said, "but you took on challenges you couldn't handle your whole life. So we gave you the afterlife to continue taking on those challenges."

"You didn't disappoint," Sues said. "Merc knew we had something when you asked for the biggest rock. That's why we gave you the mountain."

"It was quite clever," Merc said.

"And now I've got to figure out what I want to do for eternity?" Ferrun said.

The gods nodded.

Ferrun took some time to think, although he knew time was not a concept that was all that important to him anymore. His mind was made up long before he enunciated it. "I want to stay here."

The white light surrounding the men faded, and they were now standing on top of the mountain. He could see Teekola hiking up the mountain but knew the man couldn't see them.

"You've ascended from this world," Wod said. "There are countless others."

"I want to stay here and help these people until each one ascends on their own."

The men standing in front of him looked flabbergasted.

"It's impossible," Merc said.

Ferrun felt a strange sensation behind him, and he turned around. A man with short curly hair stood in front of him and smiled a light smile. He wore old robes, and Ferrun felt waves of compassion flying from him. Ferrun knew the god's name was Sid.

"Merc," the god said in an easy tone, "have you learned nothing of our friend Ferrun? He chooses only impossible tasks."

"I'll be able to influence them only from a distance," Ferrun said, stating one of the rules he knew from his communion with the universe.

"I've been watching your struggle around the world for a while now," Sid said with a simple smile. "You refused to stay in one place for long. I wish you the best in convincing others around here of the same." The man left in a flash of light, but the compassion remained.

"We'd ask if you have any questions," Merc said, "but you already know everything we do." And in a flash, he ran into the air, disappearing in the distance.

The other two didn't say another word. Sues was struck by a lightning bolt and disappeared, while Wod melted into a rainbow and arced over the horizon.

Ferrun was left alone at the top of the mountain and knew the location of every single traveler on the planet—along with their rock location, their rope length, the reason they were there, and their distance from the peak.

His mind searched out one traveler in particular. He felt her from a distance and transported himself to her. Looking over her shoulder, Ferrun saw a map in her hand. It was made out of thick tree bark, and she wrote on it with a rock that left deep black marks.

Ferrun knew Gesa would map the world, and it'd be integral to getting everyone to the top of the mountain. He smiled at her but knew she couldn't see him. He wanted her to know he was there, so he reached across the world to try his hand at a miracle.

***

Leaning on a rock in the afternoon sun, Gesa traced the points she had explored for the day onto the bark. She looked up, noticing a shift in the wind that reminded her of a life as a priestess. Instead of carrying fall leaves or a message of warning, a flower danced in the air. She watched the directions the flower danced, and it felt like hearing a spring song after a long winter.

The purple flower landed at her feet. It was delicate, and the tips of the petals curled back on themselves. She consulted her map and verified her suspicion. The breeze had carried it across the ocean.

It was a miracle that it had come this far. She smiled at the unexplored horizon in front of her. She knew Ferrun was now a god and on her side—and on the side of everyone else fighting to reach the top of the mountain.

Looking for More to Read?

Want to know how Gesa fares as she maps the world? I wrote a short story about it called The Divine Map Maker.

You can download it for free here: https://stepintotheroad.com/divine-map-maker

***

Reviews are very important for independent authors like me. If you enjoyed The Path of the Bearer and Other Stories, please consider leaving a review. Even simple, one-line reviews are very helpful to indie authors. Thank you for your support!

Also By Nicholas Licalsi

An Echo Through Time

T odd can travel through time and the multiverse. With a single focused breath, he can be any place and any time.

Instead, he relives the same day of high school over and over, knowing his sweetheart will die by lunch.

And there's nothing he can do to save her.

Equipped with time travel Todd rarely feels powerless, but his sweetheart's deaths make him question his place in the multiverse.

If you enjoy thrilling time travel stories An Echo Through Time will have you on the edge of your seat!

https://books2read.com/EchoThroughTime

Path of the Bearers and Other Stories

An AI with the potential to predict the future must uncover its creator's inexplicable disappearance. A scientist must reveal the limitations of his high profile project to while his investor takes them on a joyride through an asteroid field. A writer travels to a pocket dimension to find time to write, but something sinister follows.

Visit seedy space station bars, distant planets where dormant aliens rest. One wrong decision could ruin humanity's chances of surviving among the stars.

This book is your portal to explore the cosmos and beyond...
https://books2read.com/PathOfTheBearersAndOtherStories

Bleeding Rock

Mauve, a talented mechanic, always dreamed of leaving her satellite home. So she didn't think twice before signing up for a routine planetary survey.

Mauve awakes from the landing hanging upside down. Clearly something went wrong. She will need all her mechanical knowledge to get the mission back on track.

But the crash landing is only the start of her troubles.

With her AI assistant Mauve must use everything she discovers on this alien world to escape it.

If you enjoy science fiction exploration stories with elements of horror then you'll love Bleeding Rock!

https://stepintotheroad.com/Books/BleedingRock

About the Author

Nicholas Licalsi was born and raised outside of Fort Worth, in the beautiful but backwards state of Texas. Growing up, he was fascinated with science fiction and fantasy. This interest led to pursuing a degree in engineering and participating in multiple robotics competitions. After a successful enough career in software development Nicholas spends his time trying to trick his overactive imagination into paying the bills while he satiates his dog's need to be pet.

You can connect with me at: https://stepintotheroad.com

Get updates about my upcoming books at: https://stepintotheroad.com/signup

www.ingramcontent.com/pod-product-compliance
Lightning Source LLC
Chambersburg PA
CBHW031028260626
47153CB00016B/758